Ita Daly read English and Spanish at
University College, Dublin, where she also
did post-graduate work in English. Her
short stories have appeared in Irish, British
and American periodicals and anthologies,
including *The Penguin Book of Irish Short
Stories,* and a collection, *The Lady with the
Red Shoes,* was published in 1980. Twice
winner of a Hennessy Literary Award, she
also won an *Irish Times* Short Story
Competition. Her first novel, *Ellen,* is also
published by Black Swan.

Author photograph by Irish Times

Also by Ita Daly

ELLEN

and published by Black Swan

A Singular Attraction

Ita Daly

BLACK SWAN

A SINGULAR ATTRACTION

A BLACK SWAN BOOK 0 552 99311 5

Originally published in Great Britain by
Jonathan Cape Ltd.

PRINTING HISTORY
Jonathan Cape edition published 1987
Black Swan edition published 1988

This book is set in 11/12 pt Mallard

Black Swan Books are published by Transworld Publishers
Ltd., 61 - 63 Uxbridge Road, Ealing, London W5 5SA, in
Australia by Transworld Publishers (Aust.) Pty. Ltd., 15-23
Helles Avenue, Moorebank, NSW 2170, and in New Zealand
by Transworld Publishers (N.Z.) Ltd., Cnr. Moselle and
Waipareira Avenues, Henderson, Auckland.

Made and printed in Great Britain by
The Guernsey Press Co. Ltd., Guernsey, Channel Islands.

Chapter One

Pauline feels the edge of the bath icy against the back of her knees. If she moves, her tights rasp against the enamel, threads catching here and there on the rough bits. The air in the bathroom is cold, the infra-red heater burns the top of her head but leaves the chill untouched. There is a faint smell of chemicals and a fainter smell of drains. However, the little brass bolt is shot home; she is safe in here for at least half an hour. By that time the crows may have gone home.

She can tell from the sounds that reach her that they are still downstairs and, as she closes her eyes, she pictures them plopping on to the stiff drawing-room chairs, perching where they can, sleek and round in their grey and black mourning. She can see them pecking at the food she has prepared – bright eyes, frightened but reckless, seeking in the cupboards, under cushions, in the tarnishing brass at the fireplace for clues and hints and shreds of gossip which they may carry back with them to chatter over with furtive delight for the next week or so.

Pauline suddenly realizes that all the women in the family run to plumpness; not one of those crows downstairs weighs less than ten stone. It is the men who go, went, to skin and bones, disappearing altogether in their fifties and sixties, popping off from heart attacks or kidney failure or just sheer inertia.

And so it is today that only the aunts remain to see Mammy off, the aunts and cousin Rose. Raymond and Michael are there of course, but as the next generation they don't count. Pauline thinks that, notwithstanding their comparative youth, she has even detected signs of the male wastage in their tall, spare frames. Will Mammy's efforts be all in vain, then? Are they to go the way of the other men in the family, despite all that scientific rearing?

'I don't worry about you, Pauline,' Mammy used to address her first-born from time to time, 'you are like me – tough as old boots. But my boys are different, my boys are delicate. They need a careful diet, trace elements, vitamins, not too much animal fat.'

Pauline believes that Mammy was one of the first on this side of the Atlantic to be aware of the new dietary orthodoxy, preaching the benefits of polyunsaturates while other mothers were still stuffing cream, butter and eggs down the throats of their delighted offspring. Mammy's first cousin and childhood friend, Maureen Quinn, had married a Boston doctor who became interested in nutrition and preventive medicine and who was later to appear on BBC television airing his views, although he had never come to Ireland. Maureen wrote regularly, sending cuttings from medical journals, which Mammy read carefully, applying their wisdom in so far as the deficiencies of the Irish grocery trade would allow. It was only when Father had died of a heart attack, leaving her with three children to put through University on a greatly reduced income, that she started to throw away the cuttings unread, saying that it was all a question of genes anyway.

Which may be true, if those two downstairs are anything to go by.

In the drawing-room, the aunts sit in a semi-circle, staring mildly at the boys who slump, forlorn as lovers, on the button-backed sofa. The aunts are not in awe of them for, despite their London ways, they will always be Lena's boys. The boys resent this smiling indulgence, it diminishes their masculinity. They are cross and wish they were at home in Maidenhead and Wimbledon

6

respectively, having a decent drink with their wives and children. Instead of which they are sitting here, waiting for their sister to come out of the bathroom, in which she locked herself half an hour ago.

'Do you think, perhaps, Raymond . . . I mean, something might have happened . . .' Madge is the most forthright of the aunts.

'Oh yes, oh do.' The others twitter in chorus, raising small, claw-like hands in supplication.

Raymond stands up, pulling his waistcoat into place. He is furious now, filled with resentment and self-pity. It is typical of Pauline to pull such a stunt. How often in the past she had behaved like this, embarrassing him, embarrassing everybody. Mammy used to say it was jealousy, that she had a jealous streak. Maybe so. But today of all days.

He clears his throat. 'I'll go and see.'

The aunts nod and smile, offering little oohs of encouragement. Bereft suddenly on the sofa, Michael sets about rearranging his limbs, wishing he had forestalled Raymond and offered to go. It is at moments such as these that he must learn to assert himself if he is ever going to get out of teaching and into advertising. All very well for Raymond, big-shot consultant engineer, but why does he always have to take over? Why does he not stop to think of his brother who has taken off two days from school; much to the annoyance of his headmaster who seems to think that mothers, like ancient military gentlemen, do not have to be decently interred. Damn and blast. He stands up and hurries into the hall after his brother.

The aunts emit a sigh in unison, a sigh of pure pleasure, and then sit back in expectation.

Pauline does not at first hear the faint, embarrassed cries of her brothers. She is absorbed in her surroundings, thinking how hideous everything is. There is the plastic lavatory seat, the linoleum, the bath with its rust stains, the chain which clinks against the wall. Every

7

surface sweats, coldly and persistently, and mould creeps in cracks and crevices. Pauline had bought the infra-red heater but then Mammy had put her foot down. 'I'm not having a carpet in there, it's not hygienic, and I won't have a purple bath either. If you have money to spend, why don't you buy something for the drawing-room, a little davenport, for example?'

Mammy had seen luxury in the bathroom as a sign of moral degeneracy. It went hand-in-hand with drug abuse, abortion and mugging innocent old ladies like herself. A bathroom was not a place you lingered in. You got your business over and vacated it, smartly. Mammy hadn't approved of bath salts either, or bubble baths or unguents for rubbing into your newly washed body, or soft, scented towels to drape it in. Catchpennies, devices for separating the fool from his money. Momentary pleasure, disappearing faster than the bathwater, when there was such lasting beauty to be bought if one saved one's pennies – polished rosewood, pierced brass, Afghan rugs . . .

She is startled by the door knob being rattled with urgency.

'Pauline, are you all right in there?'

Panic triumphs over embarrassment in Raymond's voice.

She snaps back the bolt and confronts her brother. 'Do you want to go?'

Outrage replaces panic. 'I thought perhaps you might consider your guests. Really, Pauline, I don't know what you think you're playing at, stuck in there.'

'Sorry.'

Drearily, she begins to follow him downstairs. The aunts look up, anxiously.

'I'm sorry, I'm feeling very tired for some reason . . . I think maybe . . . bed.'

'And we'll be off.' Aunt Madge gives the command and the others rise. They begin a hopping movement towards the door, pausing between hops to offer comfort.

'I could send Maisie over to stay.'

'There's always a bed with me.'

'I've cut some more sandwiches, dear, in case you get peckish.'

'Yes, you must eat, Pauline, you really must.'

The boys see them into their cars, one black, one grey, like their mourning clothes. Pauline turns her back on them and pours herself a gin.

'That's a good idea,' Raymond rubs his hands, placatory, not wanting a scene.

'Oh.' Pauline turns towards him, gin bottle suspended aloft. 'Certainly you can have a drink, but do you think you should? It's getting on and you know what it can be like at the airport on Saturday evenings.'

'But my dear, we're not worried about that. We'll stay –'

'Of course we shall.'

'Until we get you settled.'

'Comfortable.'

'There's really no need for that, I'm fine. And I *am* tired. I really would like to get to bed.'

'If you're sure, then.'

'Really sure.'

They rise together, their thin frames seeming to expand with relief. They hadn't thought to get off so lightly.

Raymond places a hand on her shoulder. 'You *will* come over for the memorial service, won't you? I'll arrange it to coincide with your half-term – that should suit you and Michael, and the kids.'

'Yes, yes.' Anything to get them out.

'Lorna was so upset that she couldn't come, she was fond of Mammy.'

'Noreen was very upset too. I mean, she came over to see her with the kids last summer. I wanted her to go with Lorna to the Algarve but she was quite insistent . . .'

They are both still talking as she closes the door. Pauline pours the gin down the sink and makes a cup of tea. She makes it in a pot because she can't bear the sight of dead teabags, more hideously transformed even than dead people.

9

She takes the tea into the drawing-room where she kicks the cushions on to the floor and sits down on the sofa, putting her feet up. Then, from force of habit she kicks off her shoes too and pats the rose-pink velvet, Mammy's favourite colour.

The good-time boys are probably drinking whiskey in the airport lounge by now, though Raymond prefers tea at this time, *à la mode anglaise*. Good-time boys is Pauline's adaptation of Mammy's phrase – good boys.

'They're such good boys, Pauline, neither one of them ever forgets my birthday. And so concerned for you, Pauline, for both of us.'

Not concerned enough to hang around, though. Out and off the very week they had finished at University; settled now and flourishing, one must suppose, in Wimbledon and Maidenhead, in Maidenhead and Wimbledon.

'And I'm off too,' Pauline addresses the room, waving her teacup at the walls. The walls are newly painted, the job finished a mere two months ago, the colour, *crème caramel*, chosen after much deliberation and many sleepless nights by Mammy.

And in one hour's time Pauline will close the door on these newly painted walls. With one suitcase containing all the worldly goods she cares to take with her, she will walk down the front path and never come back.

Chapter Two

Pauline was surprised at the interest and hostility which her move aroused. Friends considered her behaviour extravagant, even louche.

'What's the hurry,' they inquired, 'the mad rush? I mean, one can understand your wanting to get away from the family home, too many memories – but for goodness' sake, rushing off to a hotel is a bit over the top. It must be costing you a pretty penny and the house can't be that upsetting that you can't stay put until you find somewhere else.'

In the hotel itself, which Pauline had chosen because of its air of hovering meekness, they wondered about her. It was owned or managed by a tiny couple who worked in tandem, never seeming to take a day off. They had neat, expectant features and shining black hair which sat on their respective heads like little caps. Man and wife? Brother and sister? Certainly Tweedledum and Tweedledee.

'And how long can we expect to have the pleasure of your company, Miss Kennedy?'

'I don't know.'

They looked askance at one another.

'It depends on how quickly I find a flat.'

'You've come to the right district. The rents aren't bad.'

'No, I want to buy.'

'Oh. Oh, that's entirely another question altogether . . . obviously long-term. We have special rates for our long-term clients.'

'No, don't bother, thank you. I must find something quite quickly.' They looked at her with a mixture of disbelief and displeasure.

Tweedledum shook his head. 'It's not that easy, Miss Kennedy . . . a major step. We can offer very good rates.'

'Really, it's fine, thank you.'

They gave up then, filing her away for future reference under Difficult Clients. From then on, whenever Pauline was to meet them, they offered her only elided smiles, eyes sliding away before they themselves skated off down the corridors that led to God knows where.

Una arrived with gossip and condolences from school – Pauline was missing the first week of the spring term due to her bereavement. They sat in the hotel lounge and clinked their glasses together. They had been friends for years.

Una yawned. 'I'm jacked.' She yawned again. 'You know, those staff meetings get worse and worse. I don't know why everybody has to shove their oar in, why they don't just shut up and get the thing over. We were there today until five.'

'Well, the first one usually is the worst.'

'And do you know our esteemed headmistress's latest idea? We are all, no matter what our discipline, we are all to be aware of our responsibility to the whole person. We are to endeavour to teach life skills to our charges, not merely French or History. Have you ever heard such crap? I mean, personally, in my life I just lurch from crisis to crisis, so how can I teach anybody life skills?' Una's rages were seasonal; she was always on the boil in the first week of term. Within a fortnight, as her coffee and cigarette consumption increased and the initial, dreadful enthusiasm of her colleagues began to flag, she would have cooled down.

'You should take another week off, Pauline, get a doctor's certificate and by then the worst will be over – we'll have the little horrors back in their cages.'

Pauline smiled. 'I don't mind going back. I quite like teaching, most of the time.'

12

And she did. Chalk and blackboard, dusty, dozy classrooms, there was no terror there. Most of her charges she actually liked, teenage girls in the agonies of hormonal imbalance. She sympathized with them, hoping that things would settle down for them sooner than they had for her. *She* had been feeling an imbalance for about twenty years now.

She didn't resent their hostility either, knowing it to be impersonal and finding it easier to stomach than the kindly patronage of the staff-room. In any case, it wasn't consistent; she knew that sometimes she was admired.

'Let's not talk about school any more.' Una waved a hand at the waitress. 'Let's have another drink and then maybe you'll explain to me what you are doing in this ghastly place. I mean, Drumcondra was gloomy, but it was a bunny club compared to this.' She looked around her in disbelief. The only other people in the room were a silent couple, sitting side by side and looking sadly out the window. Una wondered what they were staring at, for the outside world was obscured by a yellowing net curtain that fell densely to the ground, creating perpetual twilight inside. 'Come and stay with me, Pauline. I'd have asked you before, but when you said you were going to a hotel I thought you were going to pamper yourself for a bit. I know you wouldn't get much peace from the girls but they'd be better for you than this morgue.'

Pauline shook her head. 'It grows on you. Besides, I think I've found a flat.'

She was certain. It was new, that was what mattered. No memories lurked in the still-wet plaster; nobody else had lived their lives there, pounding the walls in rage or cleaning the windows with pride. It would be hers, her bit of utilitarian, undistinguished, urban architecture, warm and comfortable, two rooms on the fourth floor, looking out over the south city.

'I can see Rathmines Church from my bedroom window, and the Town Hall. And hundreds of roofs with grey slates and crumbling chimney stacks. Not a garden

13

in sight. You can't imagine how cheering I find the lack of gardens.'

It was not that she had anything against grass and flowers and ornamental trees, but she had spent too many unhappy years looking down on them, too many Saturday afternoons, too many springs when her first realization that the season had come and gone was the sight of Mrs Mooney next door cutting off the withered heads of the daffodils that grew in clumps around her pear tree.

'Handy for school too,' Una's reaction was practical. 'And nearer to me, which really is nice.'

The friends smiled at one another, embarrassed by this surfacing of affection between them. They kept their relationship brisk, except during Una's pregnancies or when either of them had drunk too much.

'Well, move in as quick as you can. Otherwise,' Una lowered her voice, 'you'll start diminishing and looking grey like those two over there.'

'They're lifers, poor things. I'll be out of here by the week-end.'

'And I'm going now or I'll start to weep into my gin. Let me know if you need any help, I can send Rory over.'

Pauline did not return to the lounge. Having waved Una goodbye, she turned back into the hotel and nodded at Tweedledee who flicked an eyelid, lizard-like, in her direction. Upstairs it was even quieter, the dim lights suggesting sleep, but Pauline had not been sleeping well. Every night she read for what seemed like hours, but no matter what time she eventually put out the light, she found herself lying back, rigid, alert.

She was still listening: for the rattle of a cane against the wall, for a voice demanding cocoa or an extra blanket. Her body could not accept its release. At such moments, in the still, dark world, she thought and sometimes spoke the words out loud – 'It is too late.' Mammy had lived too long; she, Pauline, was too old, freedom a commodity she didn't know how to use. Old lags must feel like this when they knuckle their eyes and stare at the sky, realizing that for the first time in a long time there are no bars between them and it, no prison walls blocking out the horizon.

Then her mind would switch to another image, to Mammy, yellow and papery like a Chinese lantern with the light extinguished, Mammy as they closed the varnished oak down on top of her, pushing down the hands, curved fowl-like round the rosary beads.

It was all gone. There was nothing there, nothing left to hate, nobody to blame. Mammy would never again disturb her nights or cause her to shake with rage at a throwaway remark. And her daughter was left, empty and dinged and thirty-eight years of age.

And it should be written up in the papers that virtue was not its own reward.

Virtue? Come on now, old girl. There were old people's homes, good ones, large mansions set in sweeps of green with tall trees offering solace to tired old eyes. Why hadn't she slung her into one of those? They were expensive, but then, Mammy hadn't been short of a few bob. The house could have been sold and all those antiques – care and attention could have been bought with the proceeds. That would have been the more moral decision.

But look at me, Mammy, see how well I can dance! Look at the lovely picture I've painted for you and see how my writing's improved.

Yes, she had needed Mammy as much as Mammy had needed her. More perhaps, because of . . .

Because I'm a freak. And freaks need their mammies: they need someone to blame for their freakdom and someone to love them despite it.

Why did you die, Mammy? Why did you die and leave me?

Why didn't you die twenty years ago, you old cow – then I might have had a chance of some sort of normal life.

But Mammy was dead and it was time for this whining to stop. Time to stand up straight and face the world;

time to try and eradicate from her personality that vulgar penchant for dramatization. To call herself a freak was to over-colour the reality, which was greyer, altogether less remarkable. She was a woman, out of her time, with certain things to do, obstacles to overcome so that she could attain to the commonplace.

And she would do it.

Throwing away her book, Pauline sat up in bed and jerked her spine into line. By next week she would be back at school and into her new flat. A key would be turned on the past and she would gather all her energies, focus all her attention on overcoming her – problem, for want of a better word. Thirty-eight wasn't that old, there was still time. And afterwards? Afterwards would take care of itself; afterwards would be a push-over once she had done what had to be done. That night, Pauline slept for seven hours without waking. Even though it was one of the noisier nights in the hotel, with a late-night arrival from a diverted flight, she slept on. She slept when the wind rose and tugged at the new green shoots on the trees and the foolish crocuses that had stuck up their floppy necks. She slept as Tweedledum and Tweedledee tripped past her door, arm-in-arm, heads together, chuckling. She slept.

In the adjoining suburb, Una counted sheep. She listened to the wind and snuggled closer to her husband's hunched back. He smelled of sweat and otherness, whether other person or other sex she did not know. He snored quietly and sometimes murmured, names she could not catch. Next door, all was silence. The girls were past the age where they woke at night. Lucy had been the worst; with her it had gone on until she was five, creeping into their bed in the middle of the night, or setting up howls in her own.

Lucy had been a more difficult child than Sinéad, although she did seem to be settling down at last. As a baby she had cried incessantly and whenever Pauline came to visit she would look down at the contorted, scar-

16

let face and say, 'Poor little mite, you've been cheated and you resent it. What can you expect, Una, when you insisted on giving the child an atheist for a godmother. Of course she has problems.'

Una smiled into her husband's back as she thought of Pauline's declared atheism. She was waiting for Pauline to grow out of it one of these days, though, having caught it late in life, it might go on longer than usual.

It was a source of comfort to Una in an uncertain world that belief in God was universal. From the most primitive to the most sophisticated society, some deity was worshipped. Oh, she knew that people sometimes professed disbelief (she even had herself, for a while, at University), but Una was convinced that this was because God got in the way at that time in their lives – He was an inconvenience. They didn't not believe, not really, not fundamentally. It was impossible, when you thought about it deeply enough, not to believe.

So she had pooh-poohed Pauline's objections and finally convinced her that she would make an excellent godmother for her first-born. And how right she had been.

The wind whimpered at the window and she pulled the duvet up round her ears. Rory hated the duvet but, as Una pointed out, she was the one who made the beds. She wished he would wake up now so that she could talk to him. She wanted to ask him questions so that she could hear the answers she already knew by heart. That's what marriage was all about – reassurance. It was what friends should offer too, but Pauline didn't. That was why Una always parted from her with a feeling of dissatisfaction. Pauline mattered to her, more, she suspected, than she mattered to Pauline and this puzzled her. Surely she was the one who should be the less vulnerable, bosomed as she was by husband and little daughters? Perhaps one never outgrew the hero-worship of adolescence. Pauline had certainly been the star then – head girl, good at tennis, with a steady boy-friend of whom even the nuns approved. Funny. Funny how things turn out.

17

'And funny how I can't bloody well get to sleep.' She said the words aloud, hoping to waken Rory. He snored on. Sliding from bed, no longer wanting to disturb him, she went to the bathroom and, taking down the children's cough medicine, put the bottle to her mouth. Two good slugs was a sure cure for insomnia; any more and you woke with a hangover. As she licked away the sticky runnels, she noticed that the bottle was nearly empty. It seemed a very unglamorous sort of addiction, worse even than Valium. But it was cheaper than Valium, and a hell of a sight cheaper than alcohol.

Chapter Three

The prefabs have aged in three weeks; the school, surrounded by mud after last night's rain, looks more than ever like a South American shanty town. The prefabs themselves resemble hen-houses, which in a sense they are – providing a deep-litter system for the battery children who blink in panic when they emerge into daylight, anaemic and pale. Too many children, too much fecundity. Too much fucking, the clergy would say, though in language more elegantly phrased.

The staff-room is in the main building, 1930s, redbrick. It is quieter than the rest of the school and more toxic. Tobacco smoke hangs like mustard gas, turning the light yellow, the people into spectral figures.

The spectres turn to greet their colleague, laying down pens, combs, cigarettes.

'You poor thing, you shouldn't have come back so soon.'

'You look so fragile, sit down for heaven's sake.'

'You don't look too bad.'

The concern is genuine, for each one knows or senses how frightful it is to lose a mother. But much worse, ten times worse when you haven't a husband and children to parry the blow. Poor Pauline.

When she escapes to the classroom, to the 3As, things get better. Her arrival is greeted with groans.

'We thought we were having Miss Brady.'

'As you see, I have come back to you.'

'We liked Miss Brady.'

'She was nice.'

'*She was young.*'

19

Breaths are held; gosh! Thirty pairs of eyes gaze up at her, insolent, innocent.

Pauline bursts out laughing. 'You really are little horrors, aren't you? Well, too bad, Miss Brady is gone and Miss Kennedy is back, so your good times are over. And just to show you how bad things are going to be, this morning, *mes enfants*, we are going to have twenty minutes verb drill.'

At break, Pauline finds the staff-room in a state of chattering hysteria. Helen Tierney has confiscated a note that was circulating in 4C. It lies now in the centre of the staff-room table and the teachers gather round, craning their necks and trying to read it, but keeping their distance, as if it is a bomb.

The writing is neat, legible.

Doreen Healy is too fat
She couldn't do it on the mat
Joe's micky got stuck
There was no fuck
So he's off again to try his luck

'It's so disgusting.' As Helen found the note, she is the one who pronounces on its iniquity. 'I mean, most of those girls are only about fifteen. I really don't believe they think about anything else.'

'Like the rest of us.'

Outraged faces are turned on Pauline, necks shoot out and up. There is shocked silence.

Then they remember her status, the recently bereaved. She is offered smiles, coffee. Helen Tierney takes up the note, folds it and puts it in the pocket of her skirt. The incident is closed. But not for 4C.

'You certainly livened things up today.'

Una is taking a lift from Pauline. Her car wouldn't start again this morning.

'I know. I didn't mean to say it out loud, I think I got into the habit of talking to myself in that hotel.'

'I think it's remarkable that it could have been produced by that gang of morons – I mean, it more or less scans. I suppose it's true what they say about teaching, it's all a question of catching their interest. Mind you, I don't think you're right.'

'What?'

'About the rest of us. I don't think we do, think about sex all the time. I know *I* don't. I suppose I did when I was their age, but I can't remember and I imagine that my interest wasn't quite so anatomical. The only time I think about sex now is when I remind Rory to visit the family planning clinic in case his supply runs out – you know, over long week-ends or if we're going away. Incidentally, I think that may be all over soon, I think I've started the menopause.'

Pauline feels the muscle which is her heart thump unpleasantly against her chest. 'You couldn't have, you're far too young.'

'I'm thirty-seven and my mother started early. Anyway, I haven't had a period for two months.'

'Are you sure you're not –'

'Positive. Don't even say that word. And I've been having hot flushes, so it must be the menopause.'

They don't speak again until Pauline pulls up outside Una's door. Each is preoccupied with her own thoughts, each has found a new worry. The worries, though tangential, are different.

The block of flats where Pauline now lives has been built in the grounds of a convent. There are four other blocks, for the grounds are extensive. The nuns who lived in the convent had been contemplative; they had lived surrounded by trees, shy of the outside world.

The convent is now gone and so are most of the trees, razed and uprooted by the same bulldozers. Two giant oaks remain and have given the development its name – Oakdene. Pauline doesn't think much of the name, but she loves her flat. She admires its coolness and emptiness, its simplicity. The rooms are surprisingly large and Pauline has furnished them sparingly; the floors

21

are of polished wood, the windows wide and double-glazed. There is not an antique in sight. It is half-past eight now and she is waiting for Una and Rory. She has asked them round for a drink and to see the flat, of course. She feels quite nervous, anxious for their approval.

'What do you think he does all day?' Una asks as the lift doors swish to a close. She is impressed by the presence of a porter in the front lobby, even if he was more or less asleep as they passed by. 'He can't be very busy, unless of course he's shared by the other blocks. It's rather nice having a porter though, isn't it?'

Rory, who has been dragged out against his will, yawns and begins to whistle quietly through his teeth.

'And I hope you're not going to be difficult, Rory.'

'Me? Difficult? Whatever gave you that idea?'

Una has sometimes thought that Rory is jealous of Pauline, of the closeness they share. He likes all her attention.

Rory wonders, not for the first time, why women insist on controlling a man, not just what he wears or eats, but his very thoughts. No wonder they make such excellent party members, and Catholics. They need an orthodoxy and then they try to make everyone else adhere to that orthodoxy. Rory has always found women strange and alien creatures, but highly desirable.

When they have viewed the flat, going from room to room, feeling, touching, squinting, Pauline asks them to sit down. 'Well?'

Una, looking at her hands, says, 'It's certainly very smart.'

The whole flat affronts her: the smooth walls painted in colours that are the negation of colour, the pale, stark furniture – what there is of it – the spaces that echoed as they walked across the bare boards. The overall effect, in spite of its newness, is a faded yellow look, like a newborn baby with jaundice.

Pauline is still looking at her, so she tries again. 'You've done wonders with it in such a short time. Once it's finished, it will look terrific, once you have a few pictures up and a few ornaments. I mean, these things take a bit of time.'

'It's not your sort of place, Una.' Pauline tries to make her voice light. 'It *is* finished, I don't want pictures or ornaments; this is the sort of flat I want to live in, this is it.'

'Well.'

'Well.'

The friends offer each other a smile, each equally disappointed in the other. Rory, who has been looking out over the rooftops, turns now. 'Don't mind Una. Surely you've noticed from our house that she's not happy unless she's got a pink frill round everything. She has a – a sort of brothel view of interior decor.'

At this remark sympathy flows between the two women again. Each is prepared to forgive the other her lack of taste.

'Let's have a drink, I've got wine in the fridge.'

They drink to Pauline's future and to the flat. Una thinks how much she is going to hate visiting here and Pauline wonders if Mammy's reaction would have been the same as Una's. Stronger probably. The furniture, which is mainly beech, would have been dismissed as deal. All wood that wasn't mahogany was deemed deal by Mammy. And she wouldn't have thought much of the polished floors either. 'No carpets and no dining-room,' she could hear Mammy's disapproval, 'and how much did you say you'd paid? I'm afraid they saw you coming, darling. I hate to say it, but I really am.'

And what can you do about it, now that you're six foot under? Nothing, Mammy, absolutely nothing. I'm selling your house, I may still go back and take a hatchet to those antiques. After all, I don't need the money. And burn the Afghan rugs. Make a bonfire under the apple trees . . .

Because Pauline looks so white and withdrawn suddenly, the other two decide on an early night. Una has seen this coming – Pauline has been overdoing it, rushing round so soon after her bereavement. Maybe it has been her way of coping with grief, but still it was foolish.

They say good night and Pauline has begun to hum before they are out of the door. It is wonderful to have the flat to herself again, not to have to justify its nooks and crannies. She begins to tidy away, to polish and shine. Before she goes to bed the flat has been returned to itself, buffed back to its series of unrippled surfaces.

During term time, Saturdays came into their own. Pauline made her breakfast and took it back to bed. At the week-ends she made proper coffee and allowed herself white toast – three slices with butter and raspberry jam. She munched and looked out over the rooftops. The grey slates had been turned a shining blue by the rain and from several chimney pots smoke was already spiralling upwards. There must be some early risers in flatland.

She turned on the radio for the news. No different from yesterday's, last week's or last year's: murder and mayhem in Beirut, Northern Ireland, some part or other of Africa. The body of a new-born baby was washed ashore near Clogher Head this morning; the number of Irish women going to Britain for abortions continued to rise.

Something wrong somewhere, something gone awry. Not just with you, Pauline, but with the world.

Cheered, and guilty because she could be cheered by the chaos of other people's lives, Pauline got out of bed. On her way to the bathroom, the phone began to ring.

'Pauline?'

Early for Una; Saturday morning was her time for a lie-in while Rory took the girls out to the park.

'Pauline, I'm desperate, I couldn't ring you last night. I was too upset.'

'What is it?'

'I couldn't believe it – I just couldn't believe it. I told them that there must be a mistake, that they got my sample mixed with somebody else's and they said that was impossible –'

'You're pregnant.'

'I've demanded a scan, but I know now they're right. I've probably known all along but just couldn't face it.'

'It was an accident then?'

'Of course it was a bloody accident, but I'll sue the manufacturers. I told Rory I will. He said I'll make a laughing stock of both of us but I don't care. I want justice. How dare they sell shoddy goods. Pauline – what am I going to do?'

Lying back in her orange-coloured bath, Pauline considered her body. Long and white, rather fish-like in its contours. Her stomach was flat; Una's would soon be beginning to swell. She wondered what it felt like, that little pea, beginning to grow inside. Didn't feel like anything, just made you sick in the mornings.

She had no desire for a baby, although she knew that according to her biological clock she should by now be filling up with anxiety. But that was the problem, wasn't it – she might be thirty-eight biologically but in other respects she was stuck around the fifteen mark. Like the 3As. Same preoccupations too. Maybe, eventually, if she did grow up, she would find herself at fifty, or sixty, bereft, sorrowing for the child she had never had. In the meantime, she had other fish to fry.

The answer to her problem was male prostitutes – one would do – but were there any about – for heterosexuals like herself? At least she assumed she was heterosexual, but could you be sure without having had a nibble? That's why supermarkets put on wine-and-cheese-tastings. Pauline was a great fan of these – sometimes, on a lucky week-end, she'd had a three course snack-with-wine in a supermarket. But to the matter in hand.

She would go to a night club, down one of those rickety, rotting wooden stairs to a dark basement where men went looking for casual sex and women for romance. Or so she had been told by the more junior members of the staff. Young and undamaged, they were derisive of such places, but with a bit of luck they would fulfil Pauline's need. Frequented by married men, gossip had it, which was all to the good, for surely they would be fussy about hygiene? Not wanting to bring anything home to their wives. So, safer than male prostitutes and no harm done: Pauline did not intend to play the role of home-wrecker.

She arrived early, fearing a lukewarm welcome for a lone female. But the bouncer opened the door wide and smiled a wide smile.

Inside, she got her first shock – the place was full of women. Alone, in groups, in pairs, they stood or sat around, pretty, plain, tall and short. Some acted casual, others had desperation written clearly on their carefully made-up faces. Had nobody told them? Did they not know that they would be better off visiting the theatre with a girl-friend, or out somewhere in the thick of a consciousness-raising session? Their eyes held the hopeful gleam that she remembered in the eyes of those who used to line the walls at the tennis club hops, back in the sixties.

Nothing had changed, not for these women. Nor, unfortunately, for Pauline Kennedy as she moves, gauchely, across the tiny dance floor. She bumps into a standing group, apologizes and retreats. The flush which rises in her cheeks should, more appropriately, be menopausal, but Pauline knows that it is engendered by the same rush of emotions that used to overcome her at seventeen, when she was a schoolgirl.

When the men arrive, in old-fashioned phalanx form, she can stand it no more and makes for the Ladies and thence the exit. There is something so shameful in standing there, publicly admitting one's needs, worse now, much worse than when one was seventeen. One should be passionate about one's work, or the state of the country, or world hunger, but not about men, never about men. That should be something you out-grew, like acne.

But it was, it is, it will be if only I can get the other problem out of the way.

Now that she is outside the club, her confidence grows and she remembers why she went in the first place. Technical assistance, not romance, that's what she had been seeking. More unorthodox perhaps, but surely easier to come by. She shouldn't have panicked, she should have stayed there, given things a chance to develop. She could go back, of course, but she knows she won't. There is something too depressing about those fragile, watching, waiting women. Better by far to believe the sisterhood's version of reality – a race of sunny Amazons, out there building the new Jerusalem and having a really good time playing with their vibrators.

Next morning, perversely, she woke up feeling cheerful. The rain had stopped and the sky was a baby blue. Even in Rathmines the air seemed healthy. She leant out of her window and drew it in – sharp and vigorous. Church bells rang out and somebody turned on a radio overhead. She seldom heard sounds from the other flats, for they were efficiently insulated.

In the afternoon, Una called, with the girls. She too seemed cheerful and the children wore expressions of shining meekness.

They drove to a car-park at the foothills of the Dublin mountains. There were lots of other vehicles and children and dogs and an ice-cream van that played a tinny jingle. But it was easy to leave the fuss behind. The mountain was large and wooded, with many paths. It could absorb thousands of Dubliners and did, every week-end, taking them into its greeny depths, losing them for an hour or two and spitting them out, refreshed.

The children raced on ahead, looking for signs of fairy habitation; the women ambled, at ease in one another's company, happy even.

'Who would have thought,' Una said, as they paused to turn and look down on the city, 'who would have thought that I'd be the one to end up married. I mean, you were the one with the steady boy-friend.'

'Oh yes. Brendan.'

'Whatever happened between you two?'

'I don't know.'

Pauline had often thought about it in the intervening years. She had met Brendan when she was eighteen and had gone out with him for four years. Then she couldn't bear it any more. She couldn't bear the limp good-night kisses or their fingers stickily, though inertly, entwined as they walked home together. In the end, her irritation with him had reached screaming pitch inside her head.

'I think perhaps he was undersexed.' It had come to her as an explanation just that minute. 'Anyway, I got fed up with him and stopped seeing him. I was working then, college days over, and I remember feeling very old. I don't think you ever feel quite as old as you do at twenty-two.'

'I met Rory when I was twenty-two.'

'And I met Billy Guiney when I was twenty-four – do you remember? I was feeling young again by then and I really fell for him. I was in love with him for three years and he only asked me out once – can you imagine anything so stupid? I probably still would be, except that he went to Australia. Mammy blamed me for that too, said I hadn't given him enough encouragement. She used to make me answer the door when he came round to visit Raymond, and then half-way through the evening she'd make tea for them and I'd bring it in on a linen cloth.'

'Maybe she frightened him off.'

'No. I don't think he even gave me a thought.'

He had lost interest because she had refused to go to bed with him on that one and only date. Nice girls didn't in those days, the sixties; not in Dublin, where the sexual revolution arrived a trifle late. And Pauline had been a nice girl in those days, and a believing Catholic. It was a sin. Besides, men didn't marry those sort of girls and they talked about them afterwards.

So Pauline hadn't and eventually Billy Guiney had gone to Australia, and eventually Pauline was thirty and the world was beginning to change. But for Pauline, growing older, change became more difficult, passionately though she wished for it. So here she was today.

'It's funny how things turn out,' Una voiced her thoughts.

'What's funny about it? We don't say it's funny that a hedgehog was killed crossing the road on a certain day. We accept it, it just happens; the same with our lives.'

'You know what I mean.'

'I don't.' Pauline was in no mood for nostalgia. 'Look at you. Don't you think that chance has had –'

'Pauline, how can you? I didn't know you could be so unfeeling. I came up here today to forget and now –'

The women were interrupted, and a row possibly averted, by the return of the girls.

'Carry me back to the car,' Sinéad demanded. Lucy kicked her and told her she was a baby, a big baby.

'Shut up, both of you, and I'll get you an ice-cream when we get down to the van.'

They set about the return journey, brisker now. The women breathed in deeply, slightly uneasy but wanting to salvage something from the outing.

It was pointless, pointless to dwell on the past. Pauline swore she would stop it, stop forever thinking of Mammy; stop blaming and wishing. Just get on with the rest of her life.

The sun blazed against the horizon, throwing scurrying, elongated shadows in front of the walkers. The children, diverted, tried to step on them; Una remarked that spring was here at last.

Chapter Four

On wet days, steam rose from the school as from a tropical rain forest. The air in the corridors grew fetid and surfaces everywhere turned rubbery. Chalk dust, given substance by the damp, made its swollen, gritty presence felt in mouths, under fingernails, up nostrils.

Pauline was standing at the door of the main building, wondering if she should make a dash for the nearest prefab or return to the staff-room for an umbrella, when a small figure appoached and began a circling movement round her.

'Do you want something, Marie? Stand still, for heaven's sake, you're making me seasick.'

'Can I talk to you, Miss?'

'Well?'

'Not here, Miss.'

'Surely it can wait – I'm on my way to class.'

The child's face began to crumple, her pink mouth spreading across her face like a stain.

'All right.' Pauline put an arm round the girl and led her towards a bench. 'Would you like a coffee?'

The downturned head was shaken.

'Okay – tell me then. What is it?'

'I – it –'

'Have they been getting at you again?' The child had suffered at the hands of her classmates in the past.

'Worse.'

'Home?'

'No . . . the very worst thing that could happen.'

'Oh.' Pauline sat down beside the girl. 'So that's it.'

'Yes, Miss.'

'Right, well we can't talk about it now. Look, I'll meet you after school. You can come and have a cup of coffee with me and we'll discuss it then.'

'I don't want to discuss, I just want –'

'Don't worry, Marie, I won't let you down. Just meet me after school.'

When Pauline came out at four, Marie was waiting beside her car, her stance truculent.

'Get in, it's starting to rain.'

'No, Miss, there's no need for that.'

'But we'll have to decide what you're going to do.'

'I know what I'm going to do. I just came to you . . . I wanted to know, will you lend me the money?'

'What money?'

'To get rid of it. I know it's an awful lot but I promise you'll get it back. I'm getting a Saturday job and I'll –'

'Marie, it's not the money. I'd give you the cash this second, but you can't just go and have an abortion. What age are you?'

'Fifteen.'

'You're a minor, you'd have to have your parents' consent.'

'If you breathe a word to them, I swear I'll kill myself.'

'I won't – but you see why we must talk.'

'Thanks for nothing. I thought you were different, but you're just the same as all the rest of them.'

'Marie –'

But she had gone, running across the tarmac, her school bag bumping against her fat little backside.

It won't show for a long time, she's so fat. Pauline's first thoughts were irrelevant, even callous. She couldn't take the girl's dilemma seriously; it would resolve itself as other teenage pregnancies had done. Sister Justine was kindly, Marie wouldn't be turfed out of school. She would be cosseted, looked after, the affair hushed up. Why were all these pregnant women pressing down on her, choosing her as a confidante? Pauline

32

saw the world awash with semen, none of it coming her way.

Her own fault, her own stupid fault. If Marie Gunning, fat and unlovely and barely fifteen, could get herself pregnant, then Pauline Kennedy, BA, H Dip in Ed, could surely manage to have herself deflowered.

That was it, wasn't it? Sociologists and priests worried over teenage pregnancies, journalists wrote articles about them, mothers prayed over them. But 38-year-old virgins?

Pauline started the engine, revving up furiously to get the very taste of the phrase out of her mouth. It was so pathetic, so absurd; it was something she had never admitted to anyone, not even Una. It was something of which she was deeply ashamed.

It wasn't even as if she had tried to hang on to it, it had just happened fortuitously. And for years now she had wanted rid of it. It reminded her of Mammy's *chaise-longue*. Before Mammy's taste had hardened into certainty, she had bought a *chaise-longue*. It had been an expensive buy and for some years she had cherished it. Then she realized it was not quite the thing. Over the years she had glimpsed the insides of a variety of stately homes, in magazine pictures and television programmes, occasionally even visiting them on organized trips. There was not a *chaise-longue* to be seen, or if there was it would be in a bedroom, never a drawing-room.

Mammy was not one to spend money on bedrooms, so she had set about getting rid of it. She advertised, she offered it to antique dealers – nobody wanted it, or not at the price Mammy thought it was worth. She was stuck with it. The last time Pauline had looked, it was still standing in the corner of the drawing-room. It had probably increased in value, unlike Pauline's pearl. Virginity was not a bankable commodity, too perishable; it did not acquire a patina with age, it merely became atavistic.

But what about that wretched child, what was to be done with her? Now that she had been told, Pauline felt herself to a degree responsible, particularly if, as seemed likely, she was the only adult who knew. She felt, also, a rush of sympathy for the girl, remembering the stricken little face. Marie was something of a pet of hers, which was presumably why she came to Pauline seeking assistance. She was the sort of girl who got overlooked in classrooms, being neither gifted nor brazen. Even after three years in the school, teachers would wonder, 'Marie Gunning – which one is she now?' Pauline had won her everlasting devotion when she had asked her to empty the rubbish bin one day after lunch. The child had returned the empty plastic bag and, looking at Pauline with shining eyes, had said, not very hopefully, 'Could I do that every day, Miss?'

'You could, Marie, but why should you?'

'I'd like to, Miss, please let me.'

So Marie had been assigned the task and Pauline used to meet her sometimes, smiling beatifically as she bumped the smelly bag to the incinerator.

Poor mite. And now to be landed with this. Pauline resolved to collar the girl tomorrow; drag her out of class if necessary, but sit her down, thrash the whole thing out and see what could be done.

Next day, however, Marie was not in school. Pauline made inquiries among her mates but they shrugged their shoulders and returned to their huddle.

Later in the morning she met Una.

'Come over here.'

For the second day in a row Pauline found herself receiving confidences on the same bench.

'I feel sick.'

'That's natural enough –'

'No, listen.' Una's face seemed to have grown small, her eyes larger since yesterday. 'Can I come and stay with you? I've left Rory.'

'But –'

'Don't answer now.' She took out a bag of toffees and began throwing them into her mouth; each one got a cursory chew and was then swallowed whole. 'I went

34

for a scan yesterday. I was still thinking that there might have been some mistake. There was: it's not one baby in here, it's two. I'm going to have twins.'

Pauline searched for a reply. 'It must be – it must have come as a shock.'

'Shock? It's a calamity. And that rat Rory, he told me last night – never thought of mentioning it before – that there are twins on both sides of his family, mother's and father's. And apparently these things often skip a generation, like insanity.'

'But you can hardly blame –'

'I do, I most certainly do. Anyway, he's a goat, that's what Rory is, a bloody goat.'

Pauline suddenly realized that he did have a goat-like face, with that long jaw and slightly staring eyes. She began to laugh. 'Sorry, Una, it's just the picture I have of Rory – I know there's nothing funny about it to you, but it's not that awful really.'

'Do me a favour, don't start talking about life and how wonderful it is.'

'I wasn't going to. I was just going to say that you're better off than Marie Gunning, at least.'

'I can't even cope with two, what am I going to do with four? And children are so expensive. You don't know how lucky you are, Pauline.'

'She's going to have a baby.'

'Who?'

'I told you. Marie Gunning.'

'Oh, for heaven's sake, these girls.'

'Maybe she should sue too.'

Well, the bitch! Go to your best friend for sympathy and that's what you got. It must be true what they said about old maids, sour as last week's milk. Jealous all the time, wishing it was her own belly that was swelling out. And when you came to think of it, there were worse predicaments than being married to a goat and pregnant with twins. That was bad indeed, no point in pretending otherwise, but mightn't it be worse, even worse, to find yourself on your own, growing moss around the edges and spewing out bad temper in all directions?

Pauline could have bitten off her tongue once the words were out. She smiled at Una, trying to pretend that the whole thing was a joke, but Una puffed out her cheeks, clearly offended.

'I'm sorry,' Pauline said, and she was, for she knew that their friendship was based on evasion and diplomacy, not on the telling of home truths. She had been smart at Una's expense; this encompassing fertility was beginning to affect not only her nerves but her manners. 'I'm sorry, Una, please forgive me. I just wasn't thinking and I'm worried about little Marie Gunning. And you *are* a lot better off than her, admit it now. I mean, goats aren't hard to feed and they're very affectionate.'

A group of schoolgirls, passing by, turned to look at the two teachers, legs stuck out in front of them, heads thrown back, laughing. Really, it sometimes seemed as if teachers had no idea how to behave.

Rory, who had deliberately come home late, seeking a bedtime without recriminations, was surprised to find a wakeful wife and one who smiled at him seductively over the edge of the duvet.

When he hopped into bed, she snuggled up to him, rubbing her nose up and down his spine, tickling him here, but mainly there, where she knew she would get a response.

He turned towards her. 'Are you looking for fun and games?'

'Why not? Nothing to lose now. We might as well take advantage of the next couple of months.'

'I didn't think you'd feel like it.'

'You never know what a pregnant woman feels like.' Kissing him. 'We are notoriously unpredictable, we pregnant wives.'

Oh, he had his faults, she knew that – childishness, selfishness, a tendency to view the merely female down the long length of his nose – but his broad shoulders offered such comfort, the familiar bones of his back such reassurance, that she could forgive him his short-comings. She wasn't a great one for sex but she did enjoy a man in bed: the length of him, the strength of him; even his snores could be a comfort when darkness reigned and wild things flew through the night air.

Rory, not questioning his good fortune, got on with the job. He was glad he was not a drinking man, glad now that he could strip off and stand to be admired, the torso of a 20-year-old. An extra bit of jogging at the weekends, just an extra ten minutes. Keep in shape, be prepared for all eventualities. You never knew your luck.

'Are you coming tonight?' Una rang first, mending fences.

'I wouldn't miss it.'

'We're having wild duck. I had to listen all through my free class this afternoon to how Derek shot the damn things – where and how and when. It was enough to turn anyone into a vegetarian.'

'I can't see Helen plucking them.'

'What do you think *au pairs* are for?'

Helen Tierney's *au pairs* were famous in the staff-room. They never seemed to last more than six months and Una had a theory that Helen killed them, through a combination of starvation and hard work, and then buried the bodies in the garden. She had a magnificent display of roses, and though everyone knew what greedy feeders roses were, Una swore that neither fertilizer nor manure was ever bought by the Tierney family.

'What are you wearing?'

'I haven't thought.'

'Well, I hope you'll rise to the occasion, Pauline. You do realize what an honour it is to be invited to dinner *chez* Helen. None of the others from school ever are, just the two of us.'

Helen was not the most popular person in the staff-room, exposing as she did the needs and longings of her colleagues, like a dentist's drill exposing nerves. She had a perfect complexion, a flat in Cannes and a mother who loved her unreservedly. She also had an adoring husband, and she taught, not because she needed the money, but because she found teaching worth while and a challenge. As soon as it became otherwise, she assured everyone, she would throw in the towel. Her clothes never sagged like everybody else's after a day in the classroom, and when her eyes rested on you, you felt sure that there was a pimple on your chin, dandruff on your collar.

Pauline and Una might sneer between themselves, but they were both flattered to be invited to her dinner parties. It said something about one's chic. These parties were evenings of sensuous perfection. It was not mere luxury that gave them their quality – that was only the starting point; more important was the flair and intelligence which the Tierneys brought to bear on them.

It was hard to remember any details about the house afterwards; Pauline, who had been there on half a dozen occasions, still could not say what colour the walls in the drawing-room were. It was as if your senses were so seduced on entering that you stopped noticing. You were wafted in, wrapped in pleasure: the chairs were soft but supportive, the air scented, the lights kind, the temperature just right. In summer the drinks were cool, in winter robust and sometimes spiced. The food was the kind that made you think – 'What is that flavour?' – as it slipped deliciously down your gullet. And the guests? The guests were the real triumph of the evening, strangers brought together but so soothed and reassured that they sat easy and relaxed, not an ego showing.

Pauline did not as a rule enjoy parties. Waiting to be admitted to one, on a doorstep or in a hallway, she would want to turn and flee as torn-off shreds of the frantic chatter reached her from inside. Sometimes, she actually did run away; more often the door opened and she entered, stomach churning, smile grimly in place.

None of these reactions occurred when she visited the Tierneys; or if they did, the first glimpse of Derek through the coloured glass panel in the door was enough to calm her.

Helen's husband was something of a mystery man. He was 'in business' but what exactly he did, nobody was sure. He was a large man, large rather than fat, with tiny feet and a red, rosebud mouth. Una said that it was the feet and mouth that stopped you fancying him, and certainly, although he should have been, he was not handsome. But he had wonderful golden-brown eyes that looked at you with gentle directness and his voice, like his movements, was slow and soft. He didn't say much but his listening was expressive and responsive; he called Helen 'my dear' and other women by their given names, never forgetting one or mixing them up. In his company, Pauline always had the impression that she was being conned, somehow, but it was so pleasant that she really didn't mind.

Tonight, she was especially glad to be going to the Tierneys, for today was Saturday, and Saturday nights had been designated problem-solving nights by Pauline. With her new resolve to put her life in order she was determined to go about it in a business-like fashion, devoting one night a week to what was not going to be a pleasant or easy undertaking. By choosing Saturday, she had left herself Sunday to recover, but it was a relief now to be able to take a night off without feeling guilty.

She dressed with irritation, wondering why it was that at her age she still didn't know what suited her, nor even what she liked. Helen, naturally, would look stunning, and even if Una was a disaster in pink flounces, it would be, recognizably, her style. Finally she pulled on a green-and-brown dress, more for the way it felt than for its appearance and, promising herself some new clothes, she left on time to enjoy every moment of the evening.

The Tierneys lived in Dartry in a solid, double-fronted house. It was squat, faced with orange-coloured brick, ugly, except that nobody ever noticed, seeing only the windows ablaze with light, throwing out their welcome into a dismal world.

The other guests had arrived on time also and were

sitting now, drinking mulled wine round a log fire that smelled of apple blossom; the evening was dank and unseasonably chilly.

Derek seated Pauline, placing cushions behind her back. Was she warm enough, not too warm? Was the light all right? What a very charming cameo ring, reminded him of one his grandmother had cherished. Pauline felt the pleasure of being pampered and smiled up at her host.

'I want you to meet Garret Matthews,' Derek said. 'He's taking you in to dinner tonight.'

It was part of the Tierneys' charm that, whereas being 'taken in' to dinner would seem absurd if anyone else suggested it, in this house it was just another aspect of the host's concern for his guests.

Garret Matthews was handsome, with teeth that flashed and dark blue eyes. 'So, you are the other unattached. One of the reasons I like having dinner at Helen's is because I get the chance to sit beside such lovely ladies.' He raised her hand to his lips and kissed it with a flourish.

Pauline, relaxing, sat back. This was a performance, a burlesque from a 1940s movie; perhaps he felt he had to live up to his Tyrone Power-style looks. Whatever his motive, he was obviously not to be taken seriously.

'Let me guess what you do: you edit a fashion magazine. No? Then – you run a model agency.'

'I'm a teacher.'

'Ah – brains too.'

It was outrageous but Pauline was beginning to see that it could be fun. She lowered her eyelashes. 'I suppose you are going to tell me next that there were no teachers like me around in your schooldays.'

'My dear, if someone like you had ever been allowed inside the walls of my old school, a whole generation of Irish manhood would have been laid waste. Think of the consequences for the professions – more important, think of what would have happened to the game of rugby.'

The meal was excellent. After the duck, Carmen (the

40

au pair had been introduced to the guests and had drunk a glass of wine with them before dinner) and Helen carried in two long-necked, silver swans, whose hollowed bodies were filled with fruit. Then there were nuts, and port dense as velvet in the decanter. The wine threw red shadows on the white of the cloth and the candles fluttered in people's breaths. Women smiled, men admired; talk flowed effortlessly, lazily. The atmosphere was lenitive, nothing harsh or acrid lurking anywhere. Laughter never grated but fell softly, lingering. At the top of the table, Derek watched and listened, turning his head like a cat, keeping an eye on glasses and plates and expressions.

Pauline felt the flesh of her arm brushed, almost imperceptibly. She looked down. A hand lingered, stroking her arm; there were black hairs growing on the back of Garret's fingers and his nails were worn rather long. She shivered, pleasurably. Had she then, fortuitously, found the answer to her problem?

Nights were long at the Tierneys, nobody ever wanted to go. Una and Rory now were the first to rise, speaking of babies and babysitters. The other guests, reminded of the outside world, began to look at watches; Helen hid a yawn.

'May I see you home?' He had found her coat by some magic radar and stood straightening the collar now as he leant over her.

'Thank you, but I've got my car.'

'Leave it here – I'll come back for it myself later.'

Pauline laughed, shaking her head. Oh yes, she was sure now that he was what she needed. He would make a fine playmate, just the right lightness of touch. He would be so sure, so expert that she wouldn't even notice anything; that *he* wouldn't even notice anything, which was what mattered.

'Yes, I'm on the phone . . . I don't see why not. Next week-end would be lovely. I don't think I'm doing anything but ring anyway.'

* * *

41

When Pauline woke up next morning, Mammy was sitting at the foot of the bed. She was looking out the window and swinging her legs, despite the arthritis. Pauline blinked and sat up, then threw a cushion and blinked again.

'Silly child, you can't get rid of me that easily. After all, I only came for your own good, to warn you not to make a fool of yourself. He won't ring.'

Pauline jumped out of bed. 'He will and I'll go out with him and have fun.'

'Pauline, will you never learn? We've been through all this together – how many times?'

'Anyway, it's not like that. I don't really care if he doesn't. I'm a busy woman with lots on my plate.'

As if to show how busy she was, the phone rang. Pauline picked it up and listened to the jingle of falling coins at the other end.

'Miss? Is that you, Miss Kennedy? I hope you don't mind me ringing you, but you said when you gave me the number . . .'

Marie Gunning! She had completely forgotten about the child. 'Of course not, Marie, I was hoping you'd ring. Would you like to come round, or I can come and collect you.'

'No, that's all right, Miss. I'm just ringing to say that you don't have to worry, I told Ma like you said and she's going to tell the nuns.'

'That was very sensible, Marie. Now I –'

'Yeh. Well, she doesn't want you to say anything to anybody.'

'Of course not.'

'That's okay then, only Ma wants everything kept quiet.'

Mas were causing consternation all over Dublin. Not that Pauline believed the child: her Ma knew nothing and she wanted to keep it that way – that was what the telephone call was about. It meant that Pauline was still responsible, still the only adult who knew. She tried to remember what she had ever heard about the Gunnings:

they weren't a problem family, Marie would not be considered among the deprived. Solid working class, the sort that would not find it easy to accept Marie's predicament.

And if Pauline did give her the hundred or so pounds, would she go off and have an abortion? Sex education was taught in the school, mainly, Pauline thought, on the lines of – don't and if you do, then certainly don't. Last year a priest, an American, had come to the school with a pickled foetus in a bottle. Sister Justine had wanted to turn him away but the parents had demanded that he be allowed to put on his grisly show. None of the teachers had been present but Pauline was told that two of the girls had fainted, as upset by the stink of formaldehyde as anything else.

It wouldn't appear to have had much effect on Marie, or certainly not the desired one. And still, nobody could call the little girl tough. In class she was quiet and stupid, trying desperately to understand, her round, plain face constantly wrinkled and puckered with effort. She sat in front of you, her eyes on yours, anxious, willing; her lips slightly apart as she anticipated – wrongly – your words. She didn't resent being corrected, apologizing for her slowness.

If such a child could contemplate having an abortion, then the sex education department was doing an even worse job than the French. Or pedagogy was no match for self-preservation.

On Friday, Pauline shopped late. She bought food, went to the dry cleaner's, sat on a high stool in a heel bar while a shoemaker knocked nails into pale new leather.

It was seven by the time she got home so she wasn't really expecting the phone to ring. Too late to make arrangements now, too much of the night already gone. Too late for her to sally forth either, but that did not mean she would be sitting by the phone, certainly not; in fact, the problem was how to do everything she had to do before bedtime.

She turned on the radio and began to run a bath; if the phone rang now she wouldn't even hear it.

She lingered in the bath, swishing the water around in time to the music. Afterwards, she cut her toenails and pushed back the cuticles, one by one. She plucked her eyebrows and shaved under her arms; she washed her hair. She rearranged the clothes in her wardrobe, putting school clothes at one end and week-end clothes at the other. It seemed an arbitrary arrangement, hard to tell which was which.

She looked at her watch, shook it, put it to her ear. It was ten o'clock.

It was a very long week-end. Una had taken the little girls to visit an aunt and had phoned Pauline before she left on Saturday morning. The only other phone call had been a wrong number, inquiring whether acupuncture could be used to cure migraine. Otherwise, silence. Now, on Sunday night, daylight hung about, suggesting there might still be something to do. Pauline didn't know whether she was succumbing to boredom or panic, conscious as she was of time sliding irrevocably by.

She put down the mug from which she was drinking and thought: There must be better ways of wasting what's left of my life. Having waited all week-end, she found it difficult to focus on what she had been anticipating; impossible to disentangle this time from all the others when she had sat and waited for the phone or the doorbell to ring. Surely something should have happened in the intervening years, some process of maturation should have taken place which would result in different responses from those which she had suffered in her twenties?

But she was skinned raw tonight, as she had been then, a rabbit in a butcher's window, naked and bleeding.

Silly when you were twenty-two; preposterous at thirty-eight. She felt her own humiliation and, with it, a spark of pride. She had been dishonest with herself

44

about this Garret whatever-his-name-was, pretending that she was going to make use of him in a specific and limited way, while she quite clearly had been getting ready to fall in love with him. Like all those other women in the night club. So what's new, sisters?

'This is,' Pauline answered herself aloud. 'From this moment onwards I am eschewing men.'

On the strength of her new resolution she made herself a whiskey punch, with sugar and lemon and cloves. The smell, as she raised the glass to her face, reminded her of childhood. Mammy had been a great believer in whiskey punch, although she otherwise frowned on alcohol. Mammy had been kind when you were sick, kind and cosseting. She had taken your temperature and held your head and read to you, gently, in the darkened bedroom. She had been a great respecter of illness.

When Pauline lay down to sleep, she stuck her thumb in her mouth. Less noxious, she told herself, than much of what went in there, especially other people's saliva.

Chapter Five

Pauline was now faced with a problem that she had not foreseen when Mammy died – what to do with her free time. Then she had thought only of her deliverance. 'I'm free,' she had thought as she closed the door on the house in Drumcondra, 'I'm free,' as she carried her suitcase over the threshold of her new flat.

But mankind was not ready for such a concept. No wonder the unemployed went to the bad and the newly retired dropped dead like flies. Mammy's bondage was preferable to this any day.

Now she found it impossible to believe that an hour was only sixty minutes, a day made up of a mere twenty-four hours. As she pondered the problem, she felt the penetration of guilt, for time was not meant to be squandered, particularly by one of thirty-eight. And a dull-seeming world was surely a reflection of one's own inadequacies.

In a frenzy she took all her clothes, bundled them into a sheet and threw the lot in the bin. Then, full of remorse, she retrieved them and took them to the Oxfam shop on Rathmines Road. As she looked at her now empty wardrobe she realized that her gesture had been a muddled one – giving away her clothes had solved nothing. However, it was fortuitous, for they had to be replaced. She had always believed what the fashion editors said – buy to a colour scheme, buy things that match. But how could this be put into effect with expensive impulse buys and ill-fitting sale bargains staring one in the face? Now she could start afresh and buy extravagantly, knowing that Mammy's hoots of derision as she held the price tags up to the light in disbelief would not have to be faced.

In Grafton Street she bought her new wardrobe in varying shades of brown, from creamy blouses to shoes of bitter chocolate. Everything fitted, everything matched. Then, dissatisfied with the indeterminate style of her hair hovering on her shoulders, she decided to get rid of it, cut it off.

The result was pleasing. The colour and simplicity of the new clothes suited her and her short hair revealed how finely shaped her head was, how lovely her neck. Before, she had looked vaguely pretty in an unremark- able and untidy fashion, now she seemed both elegant and younger.

Una was not impressed. 'You know,' she confided to Rory, 'it's weird, but Pauline is beginning to look like that flat of hers, all spare and colourless. Helen Tierney thinks it suits her but I don't. I think it makes her look too severe and unapproachable. That's why it doesn't suit her – it disguises her real personality.'

'You'd be surprised.'

'But you know Pauline isn't a cold person.'

'Not in the conventional sense. But there's ice some- where in that woman's body, a shaft of unmelted ice. It's what makes her interesting.'

The novelty of Rory expressing a personal opinion about any of their friends diverted Una and it was not until that night, as she lay wakeful and slightly nauseous, that her thoughts returned to Pauline.

Pauline was going peculiar; ever since that night at the Tierneys' she had not been herself. It was hard to put one's finger on exactly how she had changed – without doing or saying anything in particular she seemed to have put a distance between herself and Una. She smiled and she nodded but her thoughts were absent, her eyes unseeing, even though they looked straight at you. And, lately, she had all of a sudden become very busy. If Una wanted to stop for a chat after school or if she asked her round in the evening, it was always the same story – sorry, I'm busy.

Una was simply not convinced. How could you be busy with neither chick nor child to take up your time? Even when that awful old woman had been alive, Pauline could still spare half an hour for a chat or a cup of coffee. 'I'm hurt,' Una said to herself and kicked Rory to express her outrage. 'She's making excuses, she just doesn't want to have anything to do with me any more. She's rejecting my friendship.'

Pauline was not even thinking of her friend. She was getting on, fast, with the reorganization of her life. She had filled all her spare moments, as well as her evenings and week-ends, with a variety of activities so that there was no time left for the dangerous pursuit of thought. All the little cracks and crevices of her life had been shaken out and stuffed full of stir and bustle, and when she went to bed at night, she fell immediately into a deep and dreamless sleep.

She took up painting and bridge and joined the City Ramblers, a ferocious group who stomped around mountains at week-ends in hob-nailed boots and haversacks, covering miles of terrain in what they misleadingly called 'rambles'. She also bought a Russian grammar and tapes.

The only thing that gave her any real pleasure was the painting. She had no talent – she knew that – but she got such enjoyment from splashing on the paint in great splurges of colour. She liked the physicality of it, getting the paint under her nails. She realized too late that she would probably have enjoyed gardening.

She made no friends but she found lots of impersonal comradeship. Her new acquaintances welcomed her; they learned to call her by her first name and they asked how she was, but she could be reassured by their indifference to her response. For them, she did not exist outside the bridge club or the painting class. They were remote and curiously restful alliances.

Raymond's telegram arrived on Monday as she was leaving for school. It had been redirected, presumably by Mrs Mooney, the only neighbour who knew Pauline's present address. It read: 'Cannot make phone contact. Arriving Tuesday morning East Wall.'

Of course, the boys knew nothing of her move – she had forgotten that. 'There's no will,' Raymond had said, 'but the house is yours,' and Pauline, taking him at his word, had got the deeds from Mammy's jewellery box and handed them to the auctioneer, saying, 'Sell'. Now she realized that legally she had had no right to do this and Raymond was quite liable to cut up rough when he heard that the ancestral semi was on the market.

She decided to take the next day off and meet the boat. From the tone of his telegram, Raymond was obviously expecting it.

She waited as the cars and long-haul trucks rolled off. He was one of the last to disembark, his face set in lines of disapproval as he sat behind the wheel of his Ford family saloon. When he saw her, he opened the passenger door, then stopped the line of traffic as he leaned over to offer her a formal embrace. 'You look fine, Pauline. It's good to see you again.'

She wondered why the grown-up Raymond always managed to embarrass her.

'How's everyone?'

'Terrific. They all send their love. Actually, I have business over here so I thought I'd take advantage of that and bring the car. There are a few odds and ends I want to take back. Is there something wrong with the phone, by the way?'

'I've moved.' Leave it bald.

'You've what?' Raymond's voice bounced off the plastic lining of the roof.

'Raymond, watch the traffic. I said I don't live at home any more. I've bought a flat nearer school, only one bedroom, I'm afraid, so I can't put you up. But I've booked you in at a hotel near me, for two nights. Is that okay? I didn't know how long you'd be staying.'

Pauline heard a long inhalation of breath; she saw the hands clench and relax on the steering-wheel.

Raymond said, spacing each word, 'Let's talk about it

when we get to the hotel. If you would just show me the way.'

They drove through the city as a misty rain began to fall. Pauline directed him up past Dublin Castle, hoping to avoid the worst of the morning traffic. The streets wore their usual air of acute emergency, bags of rotting refuse leaning drunkenly against doorways, buildings falling down or half-built and apparently deserted. In the midst of the dereliction children and dogs wandered, unaware of the rain or indifferent to it.

The hotel seemed shabby too, abandoned and mean in the morning light. Raymond did not bother to look. 'Will you join me for breakfast?' He was punishing her with his formality. 'It was my home, Pauline,' he went on as the orange juice arrived. 'Father brought Mammy there as a bride. We were born there.'

'No, we weren't. We were each of us born in a nursing home in Cabra.'

'Don't quibble.' He cleared his throat and smiled at the waitress, then turned to look out the window until she had finished bringing the food. 'I don't understand why you are in such a rush, Pauline. Don't you feel anything for the old home? Why do you want to turn your back on all those memories?'

'You did.'

'Now you're being childish.'

'Anyway, they weren't happy memories for me.'

'How can you say that?' Outrage caused his eyes to bulge, like a frog's. 'You were a loved and cherished daughter, you know you were, and a valued sister to both Michael and me.'

'Yes, so long as I was there to fetch and carry and generally tidy up after the two gods.'

'Aha!' The triumphal shout caused the slow-moving waitress to halt in her journey across the dining-room. 'So that's what it's all about – revenge. Really, Pauline, I thought better of you. I always knew that you were jealous of Michael and me when we were growing up. I should have thought you would have outgrown such pettiness.' His ears and the tip of his nose had grown quite pink; he shook his head over her in sad disbelief.

Pauline signed. 'Raymond, I did not put the house up for sale just to spite you and Michael, surely you can see that? I put it up for sale because it didn't suit me to live there. It was too big, too far from school.'

'And that, if I may say so, is typical of you. I'm sorry to say it but you think only of yourself. Or perhaps it's because you don't have children that you're lacking in any sort of – of proper feeling. Perhaps I shouldn't be angry with you, Pauline, but do try to look at it from someone else's point of view. I want my son, my children, to be able to come over to Dublin and stay with their aunt, to sleep in the bed that I used to sleep in as a boy, to feel the presence of their dead grandparents –'

'For God's sake – it's only a 1930s semi, not a bloody baronial hall.'

Raymond shut his mouth and stared at his sister with dislike. 'Sometimes you can be astonishingly coarse. I've noticed it before and it always surprises me. Poor Mammy tried so hard –'

'Look,' Pauline began to scribble on a paper napkin. 'I can see no point in continuing this conversation. Here is the address of the auctioneer, he has the deeds. Go and get them. Take the house, do what you like with it. You could open a museum to the dear departed and bring coachloads of tourists over from Maidenhead every summer.'

The rain was falling steadily when Pauline emerged from the hotel, but she didn't mind. She would enjoy the short walk back to the flat. As she set out, she felt the lightness around her shoulders, like an old wreck shifting suddenly on the sea bed, unloading the debris of years. There was no reason why she should ever see either of her brothers again. Raymond was right, of course, she had been jealous of them, but that need not be a lifelong disability. Her duty was ended, her share of family piety a thing of the past. Raymond and Michael could be forgotten and thus forgiven and she could face the world, a new woman.

She was trembling at her daring. You must, Mammy had repeated over and over again, you must love your brothers, they are your flesh and blood, your kin, you must realize that blood is thicker than water and there is nobody like your own. For years Pauline had believed what Mammy said and had wondered guiltily at her own lack of proper feeling.

Now she had turned her back on all that. She had closed the hotel door on her flesh and blood and walked away. And still the building stood and still the rain fell down. Sucks to you, Mammy – there's not a thing you can do about it.

Pauline had joined a women's group to get away from sex, but she found them as obsessed as the rest of the world. Their meetings, held in a small, scruffy room over a sweet shop, always seemed to end up talking about the rights of homosexual lovers and the quality of clitoral orgasms. Pauline began to wonder if one of the women fancied her, if she pressed her hand over-warmly as she passed the tea and biscuits.

It was depressing to find that all paths led monotonously back to the same thing – S E X. It was there in the guffaws of the ramblers, on advertising hoardings, in the sly faces of schoolgirls, in Una's bulging stomach. At the bridge table, the Queen of Hearts stared lewdly at her and Miss O'Brien extended an elderly but well-shaped leg towards Mr Hanratty under the table.

Or is it me? She stared at her reflection in the bathroom mirror, then turned to range around the flat. She touched the shining neutral walls, moved across the empty space of the living-room, laid her face down on cool, pale wood. All passion was excluded from these rooms – all colour, all warmth. They might have looked dull but they were too extreme for that. There was style at work here, even if you didn't happen to like that style.

Reassured by her walkabout, Pauline sat down. These bouts of panic were something new; while living with Mammy, rage had been the predominant emotion. And activity alone was not enough to banish them, she saw that now. Perhaps she was just getting used to living alone; freedom was a heady and volatile substance to be handled with care.

As for her predicament, it was pretty ordinary if you came to think about it. It was the time, not she herself, that was out of joint. Thousands of her ancestors must have lived and died like this – millions of women throughout the history of the world. Jane Austen. Now there was a consoling thought that put the whole thing in perspective. And Emily and Anne Brontë, though not Charlotte presumably.

Cheered by the discovery that she was not a freak, not in historical terms anyway, Pauline treated herself to a scented bath. She poured herself a glass of dry vermouth and left it on the side of the bath while undressing. The warmth of the water into which her body sank and the icy vermouth trickling down her throat set up tiny implosions in her skull and she leant her head against the back of the bath, closing her eyes.

It was important to hold on to small pleasures; a glass of vermouth in a warm, scented bath. That was life, not the grand moments – which, true enough, didn't seem to be coming her way in any case. But pleasure could be sucked from the very dullness of every day, its predictability. More animal than we wanted to admit, we were reassured by routine, as we said children were. Pauline thought now that children were probably the very ones who were not in need of reassurance, who really were bored by routine. They were less timid than adults, less wary of the unknown. Pauline often looked at the First Years in September and wondered how they didn't die of terror; she would if she had suddenly found herself in their position, abandoned in a new and hostile world.

She filled her mouth with vermouth and savoured the herby flavour, enjoying the taste and the effect that it induced. She admired her legs; long and smooth, silky skin. It had always seemed to her that Gray's sentiments about Flowers Blushing Unseen were rather absurd, but tonight she was having second thoughts.

Chapter Six

The summer term was the most bearable, with its false suggestion of freedom round the corner. Even to those who remembered that September would come round again, it was easier to stomach than the darker spring term. For one thing, the children were more tractable. The exams were looming and suddenly they needed Miss. And the central heating could be turned off, which reduced the pervasive smell of damp unwashed bodies wedded to damp unwashed serge.

In the staff-room, there was an air of restlessness. Those who from time to time hankered after a more glamorous career scanned the Situations Vacant columns in *The Irish Times*; for those who were past that, the prospect of three months of freedom made one realize that teaching wasn't so bad after all, that it was a worthwhile job.

Una, looking tired, began to miss days with regularity. 'I seem to keep on picking up those bugs,' she addressed her colleagues, sounding as if she expected no one to believe her. And nobody did.

Marie Gunning never missed a day. She sat and stared dully in front of her, gnawing a ballpoint or her fingernails. Pauline noticed that, unlike the other girls, she still wore her uniform jumper. Good camouflage. Nobody seemed to pay her undue attention, but when Pauline tried to talk to her she was met with a smile and 'No sweat, Miss', a phrase so incongruous on the slack and childish lips that it made Pauline want to cry.

Sister Justine asked for volunteers to attend a two-week summer course on Pastoral Care. Everybody was suddenly busy, so many commitments. Language teachers had an unfair advantage, as Una pointed out – spending the summer in France or Germany was obviously their priority.

'Still not as impressive as being pregnant with twins.'

Una stared at her friend and wondered, not for the first time, if spinsterhood did not make one a bit unnatural. But none the less, 'What are you doing for the summer? Why don't you come down to Kerry with us – we're taking a house for the first month of the holidays.'

'No thanks, Una.' Too many summers had been spent traipsing round after Rory and Una, being discreet or obvious as the occasion required. 'I'm going to France. I'm going to spend about six weeks in Provence, painting.'

That night as Una was slopping baked beans on to plates in the kitchen, she said, 'Pauline's going on a painting holiday to Provence.'

'That's nice.' Rory had removed himself from the table, fearful for his suit as bright orange sauce slobbered and dripped from the filthy saucepan.

'It's not nice, it's plain daft. Pauline doesn't even paint.'

'Perhaps she's going there to learn.' Rory, picturing the sunshine, the good restaurants, the bright, harsh colours of the Provençal landscape, wondered bitterly what the hell had gone wrong with his life. Except for a couple of business trips, it was five years since he had had a decent holiday.

'Do you think it might be the menopause?'

'How could it be – you're pregnant.'

'No, silly, I mean Pauline.'

Rory pushed the beans from him. 'Your thought processes are a mystery to me, Una. I sometimes wonder what you've got inside that head of yours. And look what the child's done now.'

Rory left the table and Una began to clean up the mess of beans from the floor. Hot tears splashed on to the

56

beans and Una expanded into the luxury of self-pity. She didn't allow herself to do so often, but when she did, she enjoyed it.

On the whole, she felt betrayed more by Pauline than by Rory. You expected to be let down by husbands, but not by friends, from whom flowed understanding and sympathy and not mere bloody sex. Una had had it with sex – look where it had landed her. She too could have been off to the South of France if it wasn't for . . . And on top of that Pauline had sounded so damned smug. 'I'm going painting in Provence' was a real put-down when you had offered a bedroom in a holiday house in Kerry. And so baldly stated, no explanation offered, as if she were Barbara Hepworth, for God's sake.

Una snarled at the girls in turn and then snarled again at Lucy, remembering whose godchild she was.

'Go on, go and get yourselves to bed. Do you think I'll have time to wash your necks when the babies arrive?'

'The what? Oh Mummy – are you really?'

'Is she what?'

'Oh Mummy – and babies! Do you know what that means, Sinéad – that means twins. Oh Mummy, it's so exciting. When are they coming? Oh, why didn't you tell us before?'

Turning her back on the beans, Una extended her arms to her daughters. With the sureness of practice, they fitted themselves into her bumps and hollows, laying their heads on her shoulders. She kissed the one and then the other.

'We're going to have such a lovely summer, my darlings. We're going down to Kerry for the whole month. And we'll have such fun, waiting for the babies.'

'I just hope they're not boys,' Sinéad's piping treble climbed even higher at the fearfulness of such a prospect.

'That's quite wrong, isn't it, Mummy? We must welcome them, whether they're boys or girls, mustn't we, Mummy?'

Una smiled at her elder daughter, looking so like her

father in her righteousness. 'And we will, darling, we will.'

Secretly, however, she agreed with Sinéad.

Pauline sat surrounded by maps of Europe. The prospective holiday had become much more than that. She now saw it as a means of escape, her personal salvation.

She would travel overland, taking the car, because of the artist's paraphernalia. She would take the ferry to Cherbourg and from there make her way down to Arles in easy stages. The prospect filled her with unease, made her nervous and edgy. But she felt also that if she could achieve it, she would have broken out of the cringing, restricted body that she inhabited, she would be – in some radical fashion – freed.

And there was the pressing need to get away. Dublin had begun to depress her; the filth of the city and general air of dereliction seemed menacing, as if the society in which she lived was on the point of disintegration. Illiterate graffiti bloomed on hoardings, which in turn protected vast, cavernous stretches of waste ground. These areas awaited the attentions of developers, but they reminded Pauline of pictures she had seen of Berlin after the Allied bombers had done their work.

On the streets stray dogs roamed, defecating on the footpaths, so that one had to walk with eyes permanently on the ground. At street corners armies of youths lounged, their orange and pink hair bright, but their faces grey, their smiles splitting into decay.

Only inside her flat did Pauline feel safe, reassured by the shadowy spaces, the cleanness, the coolness. Even to look out of her windows was to glimpse decline. In the sterile tarmac which surrounded the flats little beds of earth had been dug out. Originally these had been planted with a variety of shrubs and flowers. The latter were now dead, choked with the detritus of weeds and multi-coloured plastic. Some of the shrubs still survived but looked yellow and ailing.

Nobody else seemed to have noticed, and maybe she,

too, needed that sort of detachment. If she could drive herself down to the south of France, she should on her return be able to drive through the pock-marked city without fear rising, as it did now, to grab at her wind-pipe and press.

'If I can stick it out for the next six weeks, I'll be all right.'

The doorbell rang and she jumped. Scolding herself for her neurotic behaviour, she went to answer it. Deliberately ignoring the spy-hole, she pulled in the door, opening it extravagantly wide.

'Good evening.' The man was fair, with an air of anxiety; about her own height.

'Yes?' Frowning, sharp, all her fears returning.

'I am sorry to disturb you. It is late to call, I know, but I've just moved in, your neighbour, and I cannot get the lights to work. Is there perhaps a caretaker?'

'We're between caretakers.'

'I'm sorry?'

'He's just left. Come on, I'll see if your fuse box is in the same place as mine. It might be your trip switch, it's very sensitive.'

Competent, gracious, neighbourly Miss Kennedy – this was more fun than planning one's holiday. The flat smelled foreign, the way he smelled in fact. Pleasant, sharp, faintly spiced.

'I have the torch.'

For a moment she saw his face illuminated from underneath; then the narrow beam had begun a crazy dance up and down the walls.

White eyebrows, quite white; and skin, smooth and polished, a reddish-brown.

'Here we are.'

They stood blinking in the sudden light.

'Jens Hansen.' He extended his hand and bowed slightly. 'You are a most kind lady and I am a very stupid man. You must forgive me – I am only a short time in Ireland and everything seems very strange.'

'Have you got everything you want – I mean, milk and bread, that sort of thing?'

'You are indeed most kind. I have everything, thank you.'

Well done, Pauline, that deserves a reward. She went to the kitchen to make herself a pot of Ceylon tea and to eat with it a dark rich chocolate biscuit. She was absurdly pleased, as if Mammy were standing there saying, 'Good girl, that's my good girl.' She knew now that the journey to France was going to be a cinch. She could see herself handling waiters – my man! – and garage hands, all along the *autoroutes* of France. She wondered at how well she felt, how calm her breathing was, how unrestricted her chest. She didn't think of Jens Hansen, any more than one would think of an aspirin when one's headache disappears. She felt self-confident and self-reliant and not all that pushed about inter-personal relationships.

She went to bed and dreamt of a pale, shining city, with empty streets and buildings of reflective glass. She walked in the streets and was surprised to find that she was in Dublin, then happy to see the transformation of her native town. She felt secure in the empty streets.

Next morning as she waited for the lift, Pauline realized how unusual last night's experience had been. Although she had been in the flat a couple of months, she knew none of her neighbours, in fact had never come face to face with any of them. She caught glimpses of them disappearing into lifts and doorways; otherwise the building seemed deserted. She rarely heard them either – no rows or music played late at night. Maybe the place *was* half-deserted, the builders unable to find buyers at such high prices. Not many Paulines and Jens Hansens, flush and tasteful, on the Irish market.

In the car-park, passing by a foreign-looking car, she gave it a pat. 'Your nearest neighbour is your dearest friend' had been one of Mammy's favourite aphorisms. Mammy had cultivated her neighbours and Pauline had fled from them, from eyes that stared and smiled and mouths that were kind but loose.

It was different over here though, here where the bull-dozers had uprooted and destroyed the spores of gossip and where the new, tall buildings had risen to be occupied by men and women of the world. Over here, she could afford to take chances, offer a cup of tea or glass of Madeira.

'Will you come and have dinner with me next Friday?' she asked Una when she got to school. 'Bring Rory and I'm going to ask Helen as well. It's really a little party I'm giving for my next-door neighbour, Jens Hansen. He's new in Ireland.'

'Swedish?'

'Or Danish – one of those countries, I suppose.'

'You're a dark horse, you and your exotic neighbours.'

'I wouldn't call him exotic, but you'll see for yourself on Friday.'

She left him a note in his letter-box downstairs: 'If you find yourself at a loose end' – crossed out, he mightn't understand it – 'If you are free on Friday night, why not come and have dinner with me and meet some of my friends – a sort of welcome to Ireland.'

She admired its nuances before she slipped the note into an envelope: it sounded impersonal but friendly.

She wondered why she was so good at this sort of thing and then thought that perhaps she had found her *métier* – sophisticated cosmopolitanism.

On Thursday night, preparations for the dinner began. The menu would consist of fish chowder, chicken breasts with ginger and almonds and, finally, marinated oranges. She thought that it sounded simple but elegant, the sort of meal that would be appreciated by a man with such white eyebrows. She began to prepare the oranges; they had to be peeled carefully, getting rid of the pith without wounding the flesh. She sharpened her vegetable knife, tried the blade against her thumb, then sharpened it again. She finished her peeling and began

61

to slice, as thinly as possible.

As she was slicing through the third orange, she noticed a red stain veining its way through the orange flesh. A blood orange. She continued to slice, watching, mesmerized, until the knife met resistance. Increasing the pressure, she felt a pulse of pain and abruptly removed the knife. Then suddenly she let it fall, opening her mouth to scream – her thumb lay now at a funny angle and the flesh gaped. In the midst of all the crimson she saw little white things – oh my God – nerves.

With her arm held out in front of her she ran across the hallway and banged on the opposite door, turning her head away from the oozing redness.

'Yes? Oh – you have injured –'

She felt herself being led inside, pushed gently into a chair.

'It's not too bad, I have seen more serious. Just wait here.'

He came back and began to do something to her arm, then loosely wrapped the injured hand in something soft and white.

'Here, support it with your hand. Now I think you should go to a hospital to see a doctor. Can you direct me if I drive?'

It was a surreal journey. Pauline sat, straight-backed, staring in front of her, fearful to look down in case the red had begun to spread over the white. The evening was clear and the light gave the city an enamelled look, with glittering surfaces and paintbox colours. They climbed a hill, then waited behind a red light before descending towards the sump-oil Liffey. The windows of the Four Courts shone blackly, its stone washed with gold.

'It is far more?'

'We're nearly there.'

'Good girl – you have done very well.'

Control yourself, stop that snivelling, no daughter of mine is going to behave like that in public. Never descend to the vulgar.

Are you proud of me now, Mammy? My thumb is

hanging off and I'm sitting here calmly giving directions to a strange Dane.

'Did you ever know anyone called Hamlet?'

'I'm sorry?'

'I was just wondering – I mean, he's probably the most famous Dane in the world. He's the only one I've ever heard of, but I suppose that doesn't sound very polite.'

In the Casualty Department they had to wait. Take your time, stop fussing, it's only a semi-severed thumb. Look at that youth smashed off his motor bike, and that woman with the purple face, her heart just couldn't pump the blood any more.

'Maybe we should go home?'

'No, you must not worry. I have asked the nurse, she said it will not be much longer.'

'It's just that it doesn't seem all that serious . . . when you look around.'

Jens put an arm round her. 'Lean your head on my shoulder. You have lost much blood, you know, and you must be weakened by it.'

She closed her eyes and relaxed against him. He felt like a well-upholstered sofa, strong yet yielding.

Jens will look after me.

She was startled by the novelty of the concept. It was such a long time since anyone had looked after her. The constant struggle with Mammy had kept them both upright; pulling against one another they had achieved an equilibrium. And then I embraced independence – and I will again.

This was nice, though, this was very soothing. She turned her nose into his jacket and sniffed at the strange, foreign smell.

'Shall I get you some coffee? They have a machine.'

'No, stay.'

He settled back on the wooden bench and with his free hand smoothed her hair. Close by, someone had begun to moan, and on the other side of the room a man, drunk

63

and bloody, cleared his throat and started to sing about Mother Ireland. A small child vomited into a green plastic bowl. The nurses, unperturbed by the chaos, wrote in notebooks and ledgers: name, address, insurance number.

Jens looked around him; it was the most interesting evening he'd had since coming to Ireland.

Chapter Seven

Jens Hansen hadn't thought that he would find Ireland so foreign. When the MD had rung from Wisconsin and asked whether he would be interested in getting the new Irish plant off the ground he had felt that it was just what he needed – a change, but not too dramatically different. He had believed before coming that it would be something like Denmark, only more backward. It *was* more backward, but it was also totally different. The first thing that struck him was the light, how it changed from minute to minute. It was never clear, even on a seemingly bright day, but soft, diffused, filtering through the swollen, moisture-laden air. Underneath, the city of Dublin crumbled, not unpleasantly, a semi but rather glorious ruin. He liked to walk in the streets, so unlike those of Copenhagen. The heart of the city was old, apart from a spattering of shoddy new office blocks, and it flaunted its decay, indifferent to the scandalized glances of passers-by. This indifference, this elderly recklessness, lent it a charm and soon had Jens wondering how anyone could ever consider neatness and order to be virtues. He found himself responding to the seediness around him. It made him feel younger than his fifty years and a bit of a devil, despite his sober, expensive exterior.

He soon discovered he was deceived; the city, like its citizens, offered more than it delivered.

In his initial dealings with the Irish, Jens had been overcome by self-consciousness. He had felt stiff and stilted where those around him seemed so easy and warm. People smiled without effort, voices were soft and seductive. There was time for everything and, anyway, there was always tomorrow. Everyone talked a lot, men as well as women, and Jens found that he could not respond to the concerned inquiries, the soft, elided glances. He was made to feel Teutonic rather than Nordic, and among the sidlers even his walk appeared like a goose-step.

Then, getting used to the place, he began to relax, to feel more confident. As he did, he was met with a strange phenomenon – the withdrawal of those around him. As he began to expand, so they began to retreat. Mouths were shut, eyes averted, faces grew troubled when he offered himself. They would have a drink in the pub with him, several even, but it never went past that. The friendliness and ease were superficial. The blandishments and smiles were there, not as an offer of friendship but to keep him at arm's length.

For the first time since his student days he felt lonely. At home, he had taken company, if not friendship, for granted. He played golf with his colleagues, went fishing with his son, took both his children to the cinema on a regular basis. He even spent a fair amount of time with his ex-wife, now that he had sorted out their differences and she had forgiven him his failings. In Ireland he knew no one and no one really wanted to know him. During the six weeks he had spent in the hotel, before moving into his flat, he had passed his evenings alone, going to bed early to read or do some extra work.

He had been surprised but gratified by Pauline's invitation, no longer expecting the sort of neighbourly gesture that he would have considered natural at home. And tonight, when she had come to him, her thumb outstretched, her face white and beseeching, he had felt pleased, almost touched. It was nice to be needed and trusted again: perhaps he was missing the children more than he realized. In the Casualty Department, as he had sat beside her, soothing her, smoothing her hair, he had felt no awkwardness or strangeness, just a sense of responsibility, and this had pleased him too.

Pauline had wanted him to take charge, asking him to

drive her to Una's house after leaving the hospital. Now he went to check on her flat. The lights were on and the radio playing; on the kitchen table there was a mound of food. As he began to sort through it, stashing some of it in plastic containers and more in a large storage cupboard, he looked around him. There were two cookery books on the table, one propped open with a pepper mill, there was an uncorked bottle of white wine and a miniature bottle of dark rum. The knife that must have done the damage was lying on the floor. He picked it up and washed it, then sat at the little table. The cookery book was opened at a recipe for fish chowder, a greasy thumb mark spread across the list of ingredients. She must have been preparing for the party when it happened, and as he thought of her standing here, he felt a sudden stab of tenderness. There was an anxiety about the preparations which moved him, as if he had inadvertently learned something about her that she would have preferred to have kept hidden. He felt her desire to please, which aroused in him a corresponding desire to protect. There was nothing sexual in his feelings and he was reassured by this. Twenty years with Helga had left him reluctant to embark on anything new, at least for the moment. No, the feelings he had for Pauline were more akin to those he had for Pia; except that Pia, now eighteen, had rejected them years ago.

Closing the book, he began to turn off the lights. Tomorrow he would have a busy day. There would be the journey to collect Pauline, and before that he intended to tidy the flat, to have everything ready for its owner when she returned. The prospect of such activity left him happier than he had been feeling for some weeks.

'It's a pity about your holiday, but at least you're avoiding the worst of the hysteria at school.' Una turned, trying to make herself comfortable on Pauline's sofa. The doctor had told her that if she didn't keep her feet up more, she was going to get varicose veins; but it wasn't always easy to find a comfortable position with your feet up, particularly in other people's houses.

Pauline stuck her thumb in the air. It was still ban-
daged, enormous. 'I'm glad about it in a way. I wasn't
really looking forward to that long journey on my own. I
could always go later – this is just an excuse.'

'I thought you were daft, but of course if I said that I'd
get my head bitten off.' Una smiled across at her. She had
been feeling closer again to Pauline since the accident.
'Where's his nibs tonight?'

'How should I know? We're neighbours, Una, not husband and wife.'

Una raised a sceptical eyebrow. Perhaps Pauline
didn't want to talk about it, but it was silly to try to
pretend that there was nothing between herself and Jens,
with him fussing around like a mother hen for the past
fortnight.

'I'm just very glad that he was here that night, and he's
been very kind since. But that's it, Una – nothing more.
Anyway, he's married.'

'Oh.' Una felt as disappointed as if she had had designs
on him herself. 'He doesn't look married.'

'That's a ridiculous thing to say.'

'No, it's not. There is such a thing as looking married –
frayed round the edges and worried-looking . . . Like
Rory. Maybe he's divorced.'

'You're not suggesting that I'd have anything to do with
a divorcee surely, a good Catholic like you?'

'That would depend. If he got married in a Registry
Office originally then it would be all right, because of
course that marriage would not be valid in the eyes of
the Church, but if he got married, even in a Protestant
church –'

'Una – will you shut up. I'm not interested in the Byzan-
tine regulations of the Catholic Church and I'm not interested in Jens, not in that way. So let's just drop it.'

'Okay, sorry. It's just that I find Jens so dishy.'

And who wouldn't? Pauline was not immune, she was
merely being sensible. You can't have him, so don't
hanker, and remember your disability.

It was one thing to unload onself on to a night club pick-up who could be discarded like a tissue once the experiment was over. But Jens was a friend and neighbour, they had talked together, laughed together. He respected her. Imagine if he should find out. Pauline felt herself blushing at the shame of it. She could picture his consternation, his disbelief . . . 'At your age?' Feasibly one could explain the situation to an Irishman, who after all would have been exposed to much the same sort of upbringing. But to a Dane? If he happened to be an anthropologist he might find her interesting, otherwise . . .

'I think I'd like to go to Kerry with you if the offer is still open.'

'Of course it is. That's wonderful, Pauline – wait till I tell the girls.'

In a couple of weeks, school would be out. The days would be even longer, eating into the darkness, presenting more and more hours to be filled. Pauline did not trust herself, with temptation just across the hall. Better to be bored in Kerry than making a fool of herself here in Dublin.

The doctor frowned and said, 'Well done, you've healed beautifully.'

'Good.'

'But I still don't want you driving. Get the bus or let the boy-friend drive you around. Nature will do the rest if you give it a chance.'

Pauline stared at her thumb, piggy pink and lineless. She felt proud of it, grateful to it, for having come through so well, despite the butchery she had wrought on it. She was pleased with her whole body today, the efficiency with which it functioned, notwithstanding her indifference to it. It was strong, it was supple; it was even handsome.

'And it will turn to dust, my girl.' Mammy stood, arms akimbo, between the doctor and herself. 'Remember that before you start getting any fancy notions about it.'

'But that's no reason to dislike it, Mammy, quite the reverse. From now on I shall cherish and pamper it

69

– even like it. I'm not one bit ashamed of it, and I couldn't care less about Eve and the apple, so go away, Mammy, and stop bothering me.'

Walking up from the bus stop towards the block of flats, she saw Jens in the car-park. He must have seen her too, for he waited at the edge of the tarmac, swinging a leather briefcase.

'Your thumb.'

'Yes.'

'So you are well again.'

'Except that I still can't drive.' She realized, standing beside him, that they were almost the same height.

'And now I have a request to ask you.'

'Of course.'

'It is to water my plants. I have been to the nurseries and bought them and now I have to leave them. I must go to Wisconsin, to the Head Office. If you could just do it once, I shall be back in seven or eight days.'

On Tuesday morning she listened for signs of his departure, then fell asleep again in the greyly filtered light. When she was dressed, she went downstairs to find the key he had left in the letter-box.

Fitting the key in the lock, she felt the illicitness of what she was doing and her heart beat faster. The air smelled of cinnamon and coffee; she began to look around at the flat which, though structurally identical to her own, was so different in appearance. The plants were everywhere, grey- and green-leaved, glossy and elegantly grouped. From the look of them, they could safely be ignored for a couple of days. She went to examine the photographs on the mantelpiece. She had noticed them on the other occasion she had been in the flat, and it was from them she had deduced that Jens was married. Now, once again, she looked at the various snaps, from babyhood upwards, of his children: the boy dark and smiling, the girl like her father but with a sulky mouth. Most of them were taken outdoors, many in boats. Pauline wondered about Danish summers, brief and therefore precious. Did Jens and other Danes spend them out of doors, drinking in every second of sunshine to store against the long dark winters?

She moved to the kitchen, where a pottery hen was hatching eggs; she pulled down a blind and found herself staring at a painted flower garden, blooming into the distance. In the bedroom she opened drawers – they were lined, the clothes arranged in neat piles. Among his handkerchiefs she found three packets of contraceptives, unopened. Someone must have told him that they were hard to come by in Ireland. And hard to make use of, by the looks of it. Buoyed up, she returned to the sitting-room and stretched out on the sofa.

It was exciting, this peeping into someone else's life, and Pauline soon found it addictive. Some days she spent as much time in Jens's flat as in her own, sitting, or wandering and touching. She imagined him wearing the wine-coloured silk dressing-gown, or lifting the pottery hen to put an egg on to boil for his breakfast. She wondered about his wife and children, and whether his wife had crocheted the bedspread which covered his bed so chastely. It was fascinating and far more stimulating than the television.

On Sunday morning, before setting out for Kerry, she left him a note. 'Plants watered. Milk and bread in the fridge. See you when I get back from Kerry.' She didn't mention how long she would be away, or anything about his trip – she didn't want to sound too personal. The bread and milk were no more than a neighbourly gesture, a thank you for his kindness to her on the night of her accident.

'When's he coming back?' Una asked, stowing the children and luggage into the back of the car.

'Tomorrow or the next day.'

'It's a pity you haven't any plants. He could have done the same for you.'

'Don't be absurd.'

'Or a cat. We're getting a kitten when we come back. The girls wanted one and I thought – what the hell.

71

There's going to be so much chaos around in a few months' time that a kitten won't make any difference. Just add another variety to the smell of pee in the house. You don't know how lucky you are, Pauline.'

The house in Kerry was a summer bungalow, damp and raw, set in the midst of fields and separated from them by a circular ribbon of concrete. The farmer who owned it lived in a more elaborate bungalow two or three fields away; they could just see its Spanish arches rising above the hedges. Twice a day he drove his cattle past their door, and in the evening the little girls were allowed to walk with him and up to the milking parlour to watch the proceedings. Otherwise there was little diversion, for adults or children, as the rain poured down.

Every day it rained, stopping only in the evening when it was too late to do anything but go out on to the step and watch the steam rising from the grass.

The children, growing bored and quarrelsome, defied Una with clenched fists and stormy faces. She roared at them, then sank back into the cheap fireside chair that groaned beneath her weight. Una's housekeeping had always been spasmodic and, as a result, chaotic; now she seemed to have given up altogether. She sat in the broken-down chair, staring out at the rain, getting to her feet only to shovel out cornflakes for the children and open tins for Pauline and herself.

The house was cold and all its surfaces felt damp and sticky. Pauline's skin crawled at the thought of sitting anywhere, or even resting a hand on the back of a chair. They tried lighting a fire, but the fuel was wet and their efforts smoked sulkily in the grate, providing neither cheer nor warmth. 'I'll do the cooking,' Pauline offered at the end of the first week.

'No, you mustn't, you're on holiday. We'll soldier on, won't we, girls?'

'Don't be silly, Una, it's your holiday too. Besides, I really will be ill if I have to face another tin of corned beef.'

The atmosphere grew less gloomy then; the children were encouraged to help and given scraps of pastry to roll out, and in the evenings they sometimes drove the two miles to the pier to buy fish off the boats.

But at the weekends, when Rory came down, the tension increased. He arrived tired and disgruntled, complaining about the drive and the weather, and Una, whom Pauline remembered as placatory to a husband in such moods, now turned her back on him or told him to shut up for God's sake.

Hostility crackled like lightning in the little house. Una muttered and Rory whistled, and Pauline wondered why Una's hormones weren't working as they were supposed to, pumping tranquillity into her bloodstream. 'Why don't you go out together?' she suggested on Rory's first Saturday. 'I'll babysit and you could go and have dinner somewhere nice.'

They turned on her such aggrieved faces that she thought: I shouldn't be offering to babysit, I should be taking *myself* out for a nice Saturday night dinner somewhere.

On Sundays they all went to Mass. 'You don't have to come, Pauline,' Una said the first weekend. 'There's no reason why you should drag yourself along.'

'No, I'd like to. It's such a long time since I've been to Mass, it will be quite a novelty.'

The church, built on a hill overlooking the Atlantic, was simple, even austere. Inside, it was crowded and a pervasive fishy smell rose as bodies shifted and shuffled, waiting for the priest. Una and Pauline squeezed into a seat, taking the children on their knees; Rory stood at the back where most of the younger men had gathered.

Pauline was surprised by the automation of her responses. Without thinking she knelt, stood, answered. She hadn't been an attender at Mass for over ten years, although she used to pretend when Mammy was alive, going out as usual every Sunday morning.

The priest was young and intense, with something theatrical in the way he presented himself. His movements at the altar, his gestures, were exaggerated, and when he turned to the congregation he raked them with feverish eyes.

He bounded into the pulpit and stood waiting, chin raised, for the coughing and shuffling to die down. Then he smiled and Pauline's heart lurched – he was so handsome. He raised his hands, white and elegant, then let them fall in a gesture of modesty and helplessness, as if he did not quite know how to begin. The congregation hunched forward.

'Friends, my dear people, another week has gone by and we have gathered together once more to give thanks to God. We have laid down our implements of toil, our hoes and our hatchets, our pots and our pans, our calculators and our pens, and we have come together to enjoy together a central moment of stillness in our lives.' He stopped and looked around the church. 'I do not want to lecture you; indeed you may wonder what right I have to do so, imperfect as I am and a sinner too. But this morning, I want all of us to dwell on the nature of Christ because by doing so we will all, I as well as you, learn to be better Christians.

'What sort of man was Christ? If He were to come down to earth today, if He were to come down to this parish, where would we find Him? Would He be on the Board of Management of Coláiste Naoise? Or would He be hobnobbing with Father Ryan and myself, sharing one of those fine dinners that Miss McNulty prepares for us?' There were titters from the congregation but the young priest did not pause. 'I doubt that very much, I doubt that He would seek out such company. For you see, dear friends, Jesus Christ was a subversive.' The congregation drew in its breath. 'Yes! I see you looking at me, wondering have I gone mad. We have seen this word used in our newspapers in connection with the IRA, and I don't mean that Christ would have joined the Provos, that He would be up on the Border today with an Armalite in His hand. But neither, I imagine, would you find Him hobnobbing with the fat cats of our society, with the wealthy, the smug, the proud and the righteous.

'Look at the company He did keep when He came down among us – outcasts and prostitutes. He didn't have much time for priests either, if I remember rightly.' The priest slapped the lace of his vestment dismissively and beneath him his flock nodded their approval of such becoming modesty. 'And that is what I mean by calling Him a subversive. He would not worry about public opinion or about authority, if He found that authority unjust or immoral. He would subvert them, overthrow them. That is what His life teaches us.

'But how, you may say to me, how can we apply this to our own lives? I don't really think that our government, bad and all as it is, needs to be overthrown.' Strong farmers cleared their throats in relief. 'Then what must we do? We must sit down and examine our responses to the world around us. Are we too ready to condemn, too ready to give approval to the opinions and strictures of somebody because he drives a Jag and lives in a big house? Do we see a man down and then kick him, for fear that we too might appear on the losing side?'

He stopped, raised his head and took a deep breath.

'Remember the words of St Paul: "If I should deliver my goods to the poor and my body to be burned and have no charity, my actions are without merit." Charity, love of one's fellow man, of the poor, the cripples, the outcast among us. Your neighbour's daughter becomes pregnant outside wedlock' – the shuffling stopped completely now that the sermon was hitting home – 'does your wicked tongue force that girl out, force her mother and father to turn their backs on her? Your neighbour's son is a homosexual, do your innuendoes and snide remarks cause him to lose his job? Do you shun him because he is different, spit on him as a pervert, instead of praying for him and maybe even trying to understand his lonely needs?

'Charity, my friends, charity and love. More important than Mass on Sunday or Confession on Saturday. The foundation of your faith.'

Una's eyes were shining as she sat in beside Rory in the front of the car.

'Wasn't he wonderful? I mean, you don't expect to come all the way down to Kerry and hear a sermon like that. At home our priests are awful milk-sops. I can never stay awake during the sermons, they'd never dream of saying anything like he did. And Pauline –' She turned round to Pauline but stopped when she saw the white face. 'Are you okay, Pauline? You're not feeling sick?'

'Yes, I am.' Pauline's voice was trembling with rage. 'I feel totally nauseated.'

'Stop the car, Rory.'

But Pauline was not suffering from travel sickness. 'I have never heard such hypocrisy in all my life.'

'What?' Una's chin slumped, enthusiasm replaced by puzzlement.

'Come on, Una, you were brought up in the same world as me, you know as well as I do that up to a few years ago girls who got into trouble would be read off that altar and their parents told to show them the door, ordered by the priests of the parish to do so.'

'But that's the whole point, Pauline, don't you see –'

'And as for homosexuality, my poor mother went to her grave believing it to be an invention of the English gutter press, as she used to call the *Sunday Times*, God bless her.'

'My mother too probably, but –'

'But nothing. It's their responsibility, they can't just walk away from it now. When we were growing up, my God, the only reason they sanctioned sex *inside* marriage was to produce more good Catholic souls for God, and now that young cub expects the people of Kerry to be dancing with joy like some Polynesian tribe when their daughters tell them they've been having it off and their sons declare that they're gay.' She turned aside to stare out of the window. They couldn't walk away from her either, leaving her like some beached whale, grossly useless and out of her element. That handsome youth should be up there, beating his breast, asking her forgiveness, asking everyone's forgiveness, instead of lecturing them on charity.

Una, who had been momentarily diverted by a vision of herself as an enlightened parent, unruffled while terms like 'having it off' were hurled around the ears of her chicks, now felt that the diatribe had gone far enough.

'That's just rubbish. You moan about the sort of Church we had in the fifties, and I agree with you. It was narrow and there was only one sin in those days, but now that it's changed and become more caring and compassionate, you still condemn it. You can't have it both ways, Pauline – that's what's known as having your cake and eating it, illogical and unjust.'

'Now you're beginning to sound like that pompous young man. I can't understand why *you* don't see that it is precisely because they are such turncoats –'

'Girls, girls!' Rory used this mode of address only when he was in high good humour. 'You are taking the whole thing much too seriously. That young lad was enjoying himself, why should we begrudge him his simple pleasures? And if you think *he's* bad, Pauline, you should have seen the fellow who was here last summer – he was preaching liberation theology. Imagine, in Kerry, where the rights of property are sacred and every two-cow farmer considers himself a member of the landed gentry. Imagine expecting them to understand the struggle –'

'Shut up, Rory, I can't stand you when you're being smart and cynical. In fact, lately I can't stand you at all.'

'I have noticed that, my love.'

'Please, I'm sorry, I shouldn't have started this.' Pauline's voice came contritely from the back of the car.

Rory, slowing behind a herd of cows, turned to look, first at his wife, then at Pauline. He was still smiling and he leant over and nudged Una before starting the engine again. 'Mind you, I admire them, they do things with conviction and panache – don't you agree with me, love? And how do you think they've survived this long, Pauline? Flexibility, that's what Mother Church has an abundance of, although She only moves when She's really pushed. But Paul – there's a guy who really fascinates me. Did you ever notice how he's always on about burning – a pyromaniac, evidently.'

In the silence that followed, Pauline wished that she had kept her mouth shut. 'Yes,' said Mammy, squeezing herself in between Lucy and the window, 'but you never did look before you leaped. And now you've upset Una, and all because you must put the blame on somebody or something else. There's a selfish streak in you, Pauline, I've always said it.'

Pauline grabbed Lucy's hand and squeezed it. 'I'll take you both to the beach this afternoon and hang the weather.'

The little girls began to jump up and down, squashing Mammy, until she disappeared through the floor.

The longer Pauline spent in Kerry, the more attractive seemed her etiolated and echoing flat. She couldn't even understand now the panic which had sent her scurrying down here on Una's coat tails. She could think of a hundred ways of filling her days, from lying on her bed, looking at her clean, crackless ceiling, to sitting in comfort on a chair that wasn't smeared with jam.

Una seemed to expand by the hour, and the bigger she got, the more she complained and the less she did in the now filthy bungalow. The little girls, affected by the perpetual rain and their mother's lassitude, sat around listlessly, picking their noses or fighting, but without much real interest. Una drank red wine, diluted with Perrier water. 'It's good for the babies,' she offered defensively, 'full of iron.' Pauline yawned and looked out of the window.

'I think I'll go back to Dublin,' she said to Una at the end of the second week.

'I don't blame you. I'm just sorry I inflicted all this on you.'

'It's not that, I just feel there are things to be seen to . . . The house hasn't been sold yet and I really should have a chat with the auctioneer.' Guiltily she looked at Una's unhappy face, the skin puffy and blotched. Pauline wondered if she should say anything to her about her drinking. But that would only drive her into hysterics – better to wait and have a word with Rory when she got back to Dublin.

Perversely, the sun broke through the bank of grey on the morning she was leaving. By eleven o'clock the sky was blue and the mud in the lane had dried to a khaki brown. There was the smell of meadow flowers and a faint whiff of the sea.

'This is what it should have been like,' Una said, banging the car door shut. 'But don't change your mind, it's bound to be raining again by this evening.'

Dublin, when Pauline drove into it, had taken on its summer camouflage. Leaves were everywhere, like frothy green bunting, hiding decay, disguising shabbiness. Even the acres of derelict sites were blooming, sprouting buddleia and long-stemmed dog daisies. Cats sat around on upturned bricks, sleek in the sunshine. The people in the streets looked different, jaunty as they sauntered along. Pauline breathed in the pollution and thought it was good to be back.

The block of flats was deserted, but bedding plants gave a touch of vulgar cheer to the outside and in the entrance hall there was a smell of polish.

Without bothering to look in her letter-box, she dragged her suitcase across to the lift. She was surprised, when the doors opened, to find someone get out. The woman, with an unseeing glance in her direction, walked towards the door. Inside the lift perfume clung, a spicy, heady scent that made Pauline's nose wrinkle. Why did the woman's face seem familiar? Was it . . .? Of course – she had seen her in a photograph – togged out in sou'wester, smiling up at the camera. It was Jens's wife.

Inside her flat, Pauline began to unpack and tidy away with concentrated deliberation. When everything was done, surfaces dusted, windows thrown open, she looked around. It was good to be back. Wasn't it? She moved a chair into a rectangle of sunshine and turned her face up to the radiant light.

A tremor of dismay in the depths of her belly had to be banished forthwith. One did not consult one's neighbour before having a wife to stay, for how could it possibly affect the neighbour's life?

Doltish female, she admonished herself, be calm, be grateful. Rejoice in the blooming buddleias, the sunshine, and your two whole thumbs. You don't know how well off you are, as Mammy used to say. Better off than Mammy, buried where no scent of buddleia can drift, no sunshine penetrate.

As for you and your pert, Danish behind, don't think you'll escape either. That will crumble one day just like mine, and then . . .

Oh, shut up.

Kicking the chair from beneath her, Pauline went back to the bedroom. She had dialled Rory's number before she realized that at four o'clock he would still be at work. Just as she was about to put the receiver back, his voice answered. 'Hello?'

'Rory?'

A pause. 'Yes. Who's speaking?'

'Rory, it's Pauline.'

A longer pause this time; then sounds of scuffle. 'Ah, Pauline. Are you ringing from Kerry? Is anything wrong?'

'No, everything's fine. It's just that I'm back in town and I thought that I'd –' Was that . . .? It couldn't have been. It was.

The giggle that came over the wire was high-pitched and definitely female.

'Yes, Pauline, I'm listening.'

If that was all you were doing.

'It's just that Una asked me to ring to say that every-thing was fine and that they're looking forward to seeing you at the week-end.'

She crashed the receiver down and lay back on her pillows, her laughter filling the room. It was too much for her, that vision of Rory, spindly legs in the air, cavorting on the giant, king-sized duvet. She couldn't imagine it as a glorious coupling, with Rory like a Poussin god, all flowing

80

limbs. His physical limitations seemed acceptable in the domestic scale of things, hardly even limitations. But on a sunny afternoon . . . And Una once upon a time had told her in strictest confidence that he had trouble with his feet – odour. Especially on a day like this. Perhaps he indulged with his socks on.

Poor old Rory. But what was she thinking of – more appropriately, poor Una.

Before she could become seduced by the scented quiet, Pauline dragged out her suitcase again and began to hurl things into it. It had probably started to rain again in Kerry, which was all the more reason why she should be there.

As she was leaving, the door of Jens's flat opened.

'Why, Pauline! Have you come back from your travels then?'

'Yes, actually –'

'I would like to thank you for minding my plants, they look very well. Oh and –' He stood aside. 'This is Helga. I should like you to meet Helga.'

'How do you do.' The woman looked surprised at Pauline's hearty handshake.

'I was just saying, Jens, I'm dashing off again, I just forgot something.' She turned to Helga. 'It looks as if you've brought the good weather with you.'

Reversing the car on the road, it occurred to her that she might have overdone the handshake. At least she hadn't slapped Helga on the back, which for one mad moment she had been tempted to do.

Chapter Eight

The windows of the bungalow were thrown open to the evening sunshine. Under the sunshine, the rooms lay orderly and clean. There were several bunches of wild flowers stuck into jam jars around the kitchen. The two little girls sitting at the table drank glasses of milk while looking at Pauline with wide eyes.

'Bed in ten minutes and I'll inspect your hands and teeth and necks.'

'Yes, Auntie Pauline.'

'I'm so glad you came back.' Una was sitting with her feet propped up on a biscuit tin. At her elbow there was a glass of homemade lemonade. Her skin glowed, pink and clear. 'I don't know how you've done it, but you've transformed this place.'

Pauline shook her head. 'It's the sun that did it – everywhere looks different when the rain isn't pouring down.'

In reality she agreed with Una; the sun had helped, of course, but it was her organization that had put a gloss of contentment on the nasty little bungalow. Returning to the slovenliness of Kerry, she had set about imposing order, unaware almost that she was taking up the role she had played for most of her adult life. Given the chaos of her emotions, it was hard for Pauline to realize what an extremely competent person she was, but looking back now, she saw that any task she had ever undertaken had been accomplished with ease. She had been as successful a student as she was a teacher; as skilled in the sick-room as in the garden.

It was only with people that she failed.

When Mammy died, she had got out fast – away from the clutter of other people's lives. But these last five days she had felt happier than she had been since girlhood.

She stooped to examine the children's shining, expectant faces and, as she did, she knew suddenly what was missing from her life – not hobbies or fancy holidays or sophisticated apartments. It was much simpler than that – it was love.

Not what Una and the girls could offer, the scraps of leftovers – that was not enough; and she knew she was past the age of giddy adolescent crushes that came and went like raindrops. What she wanted was no grand passion but something that was hers of right, where she had first claim and which she could announce to the world.

She had been wrong, she had gone wrong somewhere. The very perfection of her flat she now saw as the antithesis of love, indeed of life. No wonder Una had shivered as she had walked across its threshold. It had all the symmetry and lack of vulgarity of the grave – colourless, noiseless, lifeless.

She put the children to bed, kissing them so that they turned startled blue eyes on her. She looked at the grazed knees and the still-grubby hands and thought: This is all that life has to offer. But it is such a lot.

Back in the kitchen, she no longer looked at Una with a mixture of pity and horror. Rory's behaviour now seemed as nothing when set against the sturdiness of love.

'It's passed very quickly after all,' Una yawned. 'I thought the first week would never end and now here we are, two days from Dublin. You're not sorry you came?'

'I'm glad I did.'

'What about France?'

'That was just a hare-brained idea.' And the roads of France are not long enough nor the sun of Provence hot enough to fill up the void within me.

'Really – there's no place like Ireland, is there, once you get the weather.'

They drove back to Dublin, Pauline leading but never letting Una's battered Fiat out of the rear-view mirror. Half-way home, they stopped for a roadside picnic. They sat with their backs to the cars, dangling their legs over a ditch. In front of them stretched the Bog of Allen, sprinkled all over with the white stars of bog cotton. Here and there the peat had been cut away, leaving unstaunched wounds; the air they breathed smelled of honey and turf smoke. The children munched placidly, lulled by the silence; Pauline and Una sat, shoulders touching, flaccid with happiness.

'Mummy,' Lucy asked, 'could we live in the country – I mean, for ever and ever?'

Una smiled. 'You might get bored.'

'We never would. How could we, there's so much of it?' And her eyes looked towards the distant, glimmering blue of the horizon. 'And it would be better for you too, Mummy, because we wouldn't be always nagging. We'd have something to do every single minute of the day if we lived in the country.'

'With Auntie Pauline.' Sinéad waved her sandwich in the air. 'She'd have to come too.' Three pairs of eyes, so alike, so startlingly blue under the blue of the sky, looked at Pauline.

She shook her head. 'Oh, I wish . . .'

What she wished was left unsaid as she closed her eyes and turned her face away.

And nature, like the old trouper she was, sent a cloud at that moment to obscure the round orange of the sun.

'Pack up time,' said Una, heaving herself up, grasping the bonnet of the car. 'Daddy will be expecting us for tea, so we don't want to delay too long.'

As she drove along Rathmines Road, Pauline thought about stopping at one of the supermarkets as there was nothing to eat in the flat. But she drove past, deciding that it was not worth the effort, unable to think of one single thing that she felt like eating.

As she manoeuvred her way past the entrance gates, she saw a figure sitting on the edge of one of the flower beds. With a surge of guilt she recognized Marie Gunning.

'Hi!' The greeting was meant to sound casual but the little face was tense and white.

'Hello, Marie. Have you been waiting long?'

'A while. I hope you don't mind –'

'Of course not,' wishing now that she had stopped at a supermarket. 'Come on – let's go and have a cup of coffee.'

The flat felt hot and stale, like somebody else's underwear.

'Instant coffee and long-life cream and' – delving into the back of a cupboard – 'a pack of assorted toffees. How's that for a feast?'

'Terrific.'

Leaving her guest morosely chewing, Pauline went to make the coffee. She had completely forgotten the child's existence and, seeing her now, still wearing her outsize uniform cardigan, Pauline's guilt was tinged with irritation. What could *she* do?

'How have you been?'

'Okay.'

'You don't look at all noticeable.'

'That's because I'm starving myself. But I'll soon begin to show.'

'How long is it?'

'More than five months.'

'Oh.' Too late now to do anything about an abortion. 'And have you thought – I mean about what you're going to do?'

'What's there to think about? I can't get rid of it and I'll be kicked out at home if they find out.'

'But you told me –'

'I know. That was a lie. Nobody knows but you.'

Pauline felt panic rise in her stomach. 'But you must,

Marie, you've got to tell them. It may not be nearly as bad as you imagine –'

'No. And you swore, remember.' The blue cardigan moved as Marie's chest began to heave up and down. Coffee splashed on to her bare leg and dribbled towards her sandal.

'Okay. I told you I won't do or say anything without your permission, but you can't go on like this. I mean, you shouldn't be starving yourself for a start. It's not good for you, or the baby.'

'It's not a baby, it's a foetus.' She looked up at Pauline, her face bright with the expectation of praise at this display of erudition.

'Oh Marie, Marie, you're only a baby yourself. What are we going to do?'

'Will you stop going on? Look – I'll wait another four months, have the bloody thing and then put it in a paper bag and leave it with the milk on somebody's doorstep. You're all so fond of babies in this country, it should have no problem finding a home.'

Pauline drew back from the sudden aggression. The girl thought that the world was against her, while it was merely indifferent to her. A more depressing reality, in Pauline's opinion.

'Anyway, I only came here to ask if I could stay with you, later on, I mean, when I do become noticeable.'

'Of course you can. But you do realize that we can't keep it a secret. We'll have to –'

'That's okay, then.' Marie stood up angrily and swung clumsily towards the door.

'Sit down, Marie, and don't be silly. Of course you can stay here, you don't even have to ask me that. But you're a minor, your parents will have to know sooner or later. Legally, they're still responsible for you.'

She waited for the outburst but none came. Marie's face looked back at her blandly, but her eyes had begun to shift.

'You will come here, won't you, any time you decide. Look, this settee opens into a bed.'

'Yeh.' Marie had stood up again. 'That'll be great. And thanks for the coffee.'

'And you won't do anything without telling me?'

'Sure. Right. I'll be off then.'

She opened the door and pulled it shut on Pauline's farewells. Pauline listened to her out-of-tune whistle as she moved down the corridor.

The sitting-room was full of the child's floral scent. Pauline opened a window. Outside, the trees were covered in green leaves, concealing the gnarled branches. Bees buzzed back and forth, golden and purposeful. Pauline closed her eyes, but the images were still there – images of fertility, plashy and steaming. She drew her hand along the line of her jaw and down her neck and felt the crackle of dryness echo inside her head. Her hair hung, brittle and dead, her limbs rasped for want of lubrication. I am the only arid thing in this landscape, she thought, looking at the lines in her face reflected in the glass of the window. Arid and unproductive and dying.

Turning back towards the room, she went to pick up the used mugs. A scum had formed on the coffee dregs. She tilted one of them and watched the surface wrinkle, then pushed it away from her with distaste. It made her shudder, as the sight of Lucy picking her nose had made her shudder. She must call a halt, take herself in hand before this old-maid fastidiousness had thinned her blood beyond revivification. She took the cups to the sink and deliberately poured the dregs on to her hands. Then she let the water flow until all traces of brown had disappeared and the marks of mouths had come away under her scouring fingers.

By half-past eight she was getting into bed, nothing better to do. But with her new resolve, she felt that tomorrow would be different. She must cause a change, allow herself to flow as the water in the sink had flowed, outwards, until she met the force of life. No more skulking up here, looking down on other people's lives.

The low evening sun came through the curtains,

changing the texture of surfaces so that objects seemed to float in the golden light. The birds were up later than she, and there was the distant sound of passing traffic. She was glad of these small noises, they stopped her from hearing the echo of her own hollowness.

The summer's evening was reassuring and when winter came round again she would rattle no longer.

She awoke while it was still dark but went back to sleep straight away. When she awoke the second time, she knew it must be late, because of the silence outside.

Any hollowness she was feeling this morning she recognized as being due to hunger – she was ravenous.

Jumping out of bed and into yesterday's clothes, she found her purse and let herself out, without even washing her teeth. All that could be seen to when she'd bought her provisions.

As the doors of the lift opened on the ground floor, she saw Jens coming towards her. Her hand stretched out to press the button to whisk her upwards from his sight, but she had already been seen. He was waving.

She pressed back against the wall. No make-up; stale breath.

'Hello. So you're back.'

The bloody man was dressed like Cary Grant, in a brown-and-cream dressing-gown and matching cravat. His teeth shone aggressively.

'I too am on holidays, you see. I came down for my mail and there was none.'

'Why don't you come and have breakfast with me – your guest too, of course. In about an hour.'

She ran, not waiting for a reply, sticking her head well forward so that he might not notice her uncombed hair.

In the corner shop she bought coffee beans and milk, brown bread and a jar of honey. As an afterthought, noticing their shiny perfection, she added a basket of nectarines.

Back in the flat, she washed and changed into a pink-and-white sun-dress. Bought for Provence, it would suit

89

this morning party and reflect her new resolve. She ground the beans, moved the table up to the open window and got out Auntie Mollie's cups. As she washed them, she realized that they were the only objects that she had brought with her from home. They were hers, of course, not Mammy's. They had been given to her by the old woman a week before her death.

'I want you to have them,' she had said, grasping her niece's hand with surprising strength. 'I don't want Lena to get her hands on them. I know she's just waiting for me to die to pounce on them, she's that greedy, but I've bested her now. Take them, they belonged to your great-grandmother – my grandmother.'

Ironically, Mammy had not even liked them, thinking them coarse and everyday. It was true they were not delicate, but sturdy, with a rich blue glaze. Pauline, however, loved them, imagining them in some farmhouse kitchen where cheese and butter were being made and cream was rising to the surface of low, wide vats. They were meant for summer use and pleasuresome moments snatched from the busy lives of countrywomen. They meant more to Pauline than Mammy's houseful of antiques.

Jens arrived at eleven, looking different in an open-necked shirt. There was nobody with him.

'Didn't you –'

As she searched around for a word, he supplied it. 'My ex-wife? No, I wanted to tell you, she has gone back to Denmark.'

'I'm sorry.' You offered sympathy to a divorced person as you did to the bereaved.

'That she is gone back?' Jens looked puzzled.

'No, I mean about the divorce.'

'But not at all. We are divorced six years and it was all very friendly. Helga also has a new career, she manages a pop group. That is why she was in Dublin, not for a holiday. The group gave two concerts here.'

Pauline sat down, overcome by this glimpse into another world. Was this how Danes lived – was this how the world went on outside this reclusive island? Was there no fear as youth receded, no shame of past failures, no regrets for lost worlds?

I too might breathe free if I could escape from the miasma.

Jens sipped his coffee and took another slice of brown bread. 'It is wonderful, you know, this Irish brown bread. It tastes so good – I eat much more than I should.'

Pauline wondered why he looked foreign, why, if she met him in the street, she would know that he was not Irish.

Because of the finish, perhaps? Irishmen, even the handsome ones, often had a rawness about them, features that broke off suddenly and hair that had a tugged-at quality. Their skin seldom tanned but grew red and rough, even under the feeble Irish sun.

Jens, on the other hand, seemed smooth and rounded, his body all of a piece, at ease with himself. The knuckles on his hands looked oiled, the skin around his nails unbroken. Pauline realized, suddenly, that she was observing him with pleasure, the sort of pleasure she had got from looking at the blue cups an hour ago. She smiled at him, not recognizing the tenderness with which she imbued the smile.

But he recognized it and wriggled with embarrassment, and she, misinterpreting this, said awkwardly, 'I'm sure you have lots of things to do, so don't let me keep you.'

'You are not keeping me.'

'I just meant –'

'And I hope I shall be allowed to give you breakfast soon?'

'You don't have to, I mean, just because I asked you.'

'It is true I don't have to, but I should like to.'

Chapter Nine

Pauline was reluctant to accept that she was being courted. In Kerry, she had admitted to herself that what her life needed was love; but that love had had nothing to do with a man of flesh, whose heart you could hear beating, whose breath you could feel on your neck. Now his presence raised questions about the future and a problem that she did not dare to stop and examine.

So she chided herself, reminding herself of the importance of friendship, as she looked at her reflection in the bathroom mirror. 'Men are only men,' she spoke sternly. 'Less than half the world, after all.' And she wished for longer hair, firmer breasts, younger skin.

She tried to fight back the happiness that sucked her into its treacherous swamp, but no matter how often she reminded herself of its transience, of life's brevity, it made no difference. The present triumphed and she smiled getting up in the morning and going to bed at night.

Now she pitied Una and Rory, trapped in a marriage contracted when they were mere babes; now she saw the luck of her own life, a heart intact except for some surface scratches, a whole new world to be explored as she stood at the mouth of middle age. She no longer marvelled at Helga's spectacular career – her own miracle made that seem a commonplace. For the first time in twenty years she prayed to God, not for a continuance of her happiness, but to keep Jens safe. Please, let him not be run over by a bus or smashed to pieces in his BMW. Let him not be mugged at night, or fall into the Liffey or develop cancer.

When they parted at their doors and said good night, she listened for the click of his lock and only then turned her own.

And it's not a romance, she told herself, having at last admitted that they had begun to see one another on a regular basis. It's not a romance, mere friendship between two mature people. No commitments; he hasn't kissed me; there's no need to worry about the future, which is never going to come about anyway.

The weather was kind, the sun shone and, both children of the cold North, they asked for no more but turned their faces to its rays, unhunching their shoulders. They sat on park benches, walked under dusty city trees, offered bread to the sated ducks in Stephen's Green. When it rained, they went to the pictures. The half-empty cinemas smelled of stale perfume and tobacco. The scattered patrons, deep in their Pullman seats, expelled air from their lungs in deep sighs and looked at the flickering screen. Afterwards, Pauline could never remember anything about the film though she could tell you, if asked, how many times Jens had yawned or stretched, or brushed her arm with his hand, so near there in the darkness. She had never realized how obsessed one could become with another person: she knew what his knuckles looked like, the shape of his ear. If she were in a crowded room with her eyes closed and he were to clear this throat in a far corner, she would have recognized instantly that rattle of phlegm as his.

In their block of flats many people were on holiday. The car-park was half-empty and inside the building the silence seemed more profound. During the day they were the only two around. They left their front doors open, creating an impression of airiness and space, and when the sun shone through the open windows, the light flooded the beige interiors, transforming them into sparkling singing chambers.

It was an enchantment, and by their nature enchantments cannot last. But who was caring? Who was counting? Not Pauline, with Mammy back securely in her box and life extending only to the now. Not Jens, who'd had his fill of love but was pleased that this pretty lady had come along. She was uncomplicated and undemanding and he didn't feel uptight. Things would develop in their own time; if not, no harm done.

Una phoned: 'I know I can't compete with the glamorous Dane but could you give an old friend a ring?'

'I'm sorry, Una. You know how it is.'

'I can't remember that far back.'

Una had spread since their return from Kerry. She trundled towards the kitchen in front of Pauline, swaying in an effort to stabilize her bulk. 'I've been eating like a pig and my blood pressure is up,' she said, heaving herself on to a chair. 'These children are going to kill me, I know it.'

'Don't make jokes like that.'

'I'm not joking. Do you believe in dreams, Pauline? I've been having this awful nightmare. I'm lying there just as the second one slides into the world. I hear the plop and feel the slime around my thighs, and then I can't breathe. I'm fighting for breath and I hear a nurse say, "She's sinking fast," and then I wake up.'

'But it's just a dream, Una.'

'And when I wake up I still can't breathe. So I lie there, fighting down the panic, and then I turn to that bugger and he's snoring away like one of the seven dwarfs, and I get into such a frenzy that I can't get back to sleep for the rest of the night. You don't know how lucky you are to have escaped all this.'

'Oh – so you don't hold out much hope for Jens and myself?' Pauline offered this as a distraction, without seriousness, but Una heard only the words, not the tone in which they were offered. She half-rose from the chair, her face shining. 'I knew it, Pauline – I knew it. How wonderful. I'm so glad. Are you going to have a ring?'

'Una – that was a joke.'

'I know he's mad about you, I could see that right away.'

'It *was* a joke, really. And anyway, you're not very consistent, are you? One minute you're congratulating me on having avoided the holy state, and the next you're falling around the place with delight because you think I'm getting married.'

'You don't have to keep it a secret from me – it's not as if I'm going to rush off and tell the rest of the staff.'

'For the last time, there's nothing to tell. There is friendship between us, nothing more. I don't want anything more.'

Una smiled her disbelief. 'Of course you don't. I must say, though, friendship is good for the system – you look ten years younger than you did this time last year. Keep taking the medicine, that's my advice, Pauline, whatever the brand-name.'

Denmark was the enemy. She saw it as a cold, bleak land, whose icy waters tore at its shores, leaving it gashed and ugly. She imagined it dark and primevally wooded and she visualized Jens one day disappearing into its endless winter. She would never see him again. He would vanish, slip from her loving gaze and be turned into a frog by a wicked Viking troll with a long blond beard and pointed ears.

If only he were Irish.

But he wouldn't be available then, not handsome Jens. He would be married, dancing the night away in some Leeson Street night club, returning to the conubial bed well pleased with himself and his ability to have his cake and eat it.

'Try not to make a fool of yourself, at your age.' Mammy had taken to nightly visits, looking over Pauline's shoulder as she patted moisturizing lotion on to her face in front of the dressing-table mirror. 'There's no fool like an old fool, but really, you're an intelligent woman. I didn't think you'd be so gullible.'

'I'm not looking for your approval, that's all over, Mammy, so stop ranting.'

'Then you *are* gullible. Imagine wasting your money

on that rubbish. Collagen – what will they come up with next? Look at my skin – nothing but soap and water all my life, but then, unfortunately, you took after the Kennedys in that respect.'

Although Pauline feared that she *was* making a fool of herself, increasingly she didn't care. Now when she was in his presence, she found herself overwhelmed with sexual desire. It was an effort not to reach out and touch him. She grew weak listening to his voice, not taking in the sense; conscious only of her need to feel his skin, to rub her body against his, to suck him like a soother until saturation point and then to lie beside him, for ever.

If he kisses me now, she'd think, turning her face from him to hide its nakedness, if he kisses me now there will be no problem, it will all happen quite naturally, he won't even notice anything.

But he didn't kiss her. She watched his lips move as he enunciated his slightly peculiar English, but they never drew near hers. His teeth were white and even, and visible when he talked; at the crown of his head his blond hair had begun to thin, and even that she found attractive.

'Would you like to show me your country? We could go away for a few days together.'

'What? What?' Not listening and then not believing what she heard.

'Before I go back to work. I should like to see the countryside, away from the city for a change.'

She took him inland, to the flat central plain, less spectacular than the coast but quieter also. It was rich, domesticated countryside where trees had been planted and fields tilled for hundreds of years. The roads were white and obscured by tall, effusive hedges; the villages through which they passed were deserted, far stiller than the countryside around them.

They parked the car at the edge of one of them and went to explore its streets. They passed by a terrace of fine, eighteenth-century houses, their fanlights and wrought-iron railings still intact. At a sweet shop they bought ice-cream cones and dawdled outside, eating them in the sunshine. There were coloured glass dispensing bottles in the window of the Medical Hall, and in that of T. Dunne, Hardware Store, a cat slept, curled up among boxes of nails and green plastic watering-cans.

Nobody moved along the whole length of the street. The lime trees at the end near the derelict Protestant church shifted slightly, giving Pauline sudden vertigo. If I faint now, she thought, what will happen? Will someone rush from the Medical Hall to offer me assistance? Will Jens realize it is a weakness brought on by love?

But as she swayed, he took her arm. 'It's so hot. I didn't know you got such summers in Ireland.'

'Only in the midlands – there's never any wind in the midlands.'

The street forked and, turning left, they came upon Flood's Commercial Hotel.

'We could stay here.' Jens looked up at its dour façade with hesitation. 'At least, I don't imagine it's booked out.'

They waited in the gloomy hall under a plastic sign which read Reception. There was no bell to ring, no counter to bang, but eventually, after some foot-stamping, a door opened and a woman's head appeared. 'Yes?'

'We would like to stay, please.'

She emerged, tying her floral overall behind her. 'You caught me on the hop. I didn't expect anyone at all at this time of day.'

Pauline listened as Jens asked for two single rooms, wondering whether the feeling which spread throughout her body was one of relief or disappointment.

'I can't give ye dinner now, it's too late, but would ye care for tea?' The woman led the way along a corridor that smelled of fried onions. 'Now, I'll get some sandwiches too. And leave your bags. One of the lads will bring them up later.'

The dining-room was dusty, the air scented with the faint musk of geraniums. There was an upright piano in one corner and a cluster of sauce bottles on each table. On a vast sideboard, running the length of the wall, there were several rows of silver cups. Peering, Pauline read that they had been won for Irish dancing and Gaelic football.

Despite the sauce bottles, it seemed unlikely that anyone had ever eaten a meal in the room.

The tea was strong and the sandwiches slices of crusty bread filled with slabs of roast beef.

'We don't have many people staying,' the woman said, as she set the cups in front of them. 'Maybe things will improve though, now that the weather's so fine.'

She sounded wistful and Pauline smiled encouragingly. 'I'm sure they will – it's so pretty around here.'

'Isn't it now. That's what I always say, if people only knew.'

When they had eaten, they went out again into the sunshine. A river, swift-flowing and wide, skirted the town. It flowed into flat green fields for there was no rise in the land. Everywhere there were great ancient trees, affording giant archways of shade, and, they imagined, totally weatherproof. In the fields around them crops ripened and tow-headed farmers rode their tractors like steeds. The landscape spoke of order, careful cultivation and sobriety. It felt as if it had been lived in for generations, shining with good nature and attention.

'It's very un-Irish,' Pauline told Jens.

'Is it?'

'Yes, it's not bleak and harrowing and romantic like so much of the country – it's just ordinary and pretty. That's why I like it so much. I can't bear the drama of places like Kerry and Connemara. You get a surfeit of drama if you live in Ireland for long.'

* * *

That night they slept in their single rooms, on either side of an enormous bathroom whose plumbing rumbled sporadically. In the morning they set out for a walk, and that was to be the pattern of their holiday – taking strolls every day, following the course of the river or forsaking it for the wider fields, their pockets stuffed with apples and oranges.

In the evenings they drank whiskey in the Cocktail Lounge, where Mrs Flood presided, without her overall now, and elegant in lipstick and frilled nylon blouses.

One day, following the river, they came to a canal that flowed into it. Taking the tow-path, they walked on until they reached a large basin of water, where the canal ended. It was a miniature harbour, set in the middle of nowhere.

'Is it real?' Pauline blinked, not sure that she wasn't hallucinating under the hot and scented air.

'Quite real but very strange.'

They sat down, pressing against the hedge for shade. Above their heads the bees worked, flying in and out, shaking the petals of woodbine and wild rose and releasing a headier perfume. There was a heat gloss everywhere, on leaves, on stones, on water. Pauline closed her eyes and felt relief at the sudden golden shade.

'Look,' Jens said.

Pauline shook her head. 'It's too dazzling.'

'But there's a house over there – I can see smoke behind those trees.'

'You're imagining things. How could there be a house here when there isn't even a road?'

Grasping her hand, Jens pulled her up.

They skirted the basin. 'Look – a boat.' Leading up from where the boat was moored they could make out a rough pathway, with grass flattened and cow parsley and nettles beaten back. The path ended at a gap in a tall hedge and through this they saw the house – a small, square cottage sitting there in the middle of a field.

'Well, hello.'

They heard the voice but couldn't see the woman at

first as she stood in the darkness behind the open front door. Then she stepped, squinting, into the sunshine.

'You're just in time for tea.' She seemed quite unsurprised by their sudden appearance, placing a tray she was carrying down on a card table. 'Now, my only problem is I've no sugar. As I don't use it myself I cannot be bothered buying it in the shop. You'd be surprised how heavy a bag of sugar is. Do either of you take sugar?'

She smiled at them and the smile broadened as they shook their heads.

'Then all we need are some more cups, and Bob's your uncle.' She waddled back inside, manoeuvring her hips sideways through the door. There was a plate of scones on the tray and a honeycomb, sticky on a saucer.

'It's very kind of you –'

'Maisie. Maisie is the name, dear. And not kind at all. It's a red-letter day for me when somebody drops in for tea. It can get lonely here, although not too bad in the summer. You'd be surprised the number of visitors I get dropping by. They leave their motor on the Birr road and go exploring. More often than not they end up here. Is that what you did, dear?'

'We actually –'

'That's right, dear. Now have a scone, both of you – you could do with a bit of fattening up. Married, are you?'

'No, we're –'

'None of your business, Maisie, though to tell you the truth I'm not nosy. Not like the Irish. My husband, Hughie, he was Irish and even though he lived off the Whitechapel Road for thirty years he never lost that habit. Strange that – after all those years in London, nosiness and Ireland, they was his only hobbies.

'That's what has me here, dears – the Irishness, I mean, not the nosiness. I'd still be living off the Whitechapel Road, I dare say, if it wasn't for that man always going on about Ireland.'

It was a tale of devotion. Hughie Byrne had left

101

Ireland and gone to England just as the war was ending. There he had met and married Maisie and for almost thirty years they had lived in that great city. First they had rented a room, but after five years they had got a council flat. There were no children but they were happy, going to the pub on a Saturday night and to bingo on a Wednesday. At Easter and Christmas Hughie took Maisie to Mass, although he had lost interest in that once they introduced long-haired louts with guitars in place of a proper choir. He had never lost his affection for Ireland though. Over a cup of tea in bed on a Sunday morning or sitting together finishing their stout after the telly had gone off, he had told Maisie about the land where he had been born and reared. He had spoken of his family, the two-roomed cottage where they had been brought up; of walking to school five miles every morning and stopping at the crossroads on the way back for a game of pitch and toss.

Even when he spoke of the hard times, his eyes were moist with love and Maisie would say, 'Why don't we go back, Hughie? Why don't you and me take a holiday over the water?'

But he never would. Maisie had wondered why. They could have saved for the fare, it wasn't that much on the boat. When she'd say this to him, he would simply shake his head and then, rubbing his hands briskly together, suggest an outing to the Rose and Crown.

'And then he died and I said to myself – because you can't talk to a corpse – I said, "Hughie Byrne, I can't bury you in this country, you'd never rest easy if I did. I'll take you home, even if it costs a few bob." '

And it had, more than a few bob. She had had to sell all her belongings, after she had borrowed fifty quid from the money-lenders on their security. Then she and the lead coffin had left Heathrow Airport on an Aer Lingus plane. She had never flown before or since.

'So I couldn't go back to London then – could I, dears? Where would I find fifty quid to pay back those sharks and, if I didn't cough up, it would have been curtains for

102

Maisie. So I stayed on here. His relations was very nice to me, cousins and that, but I couldn't stay with them for ever. So I got this little house eventually and I'm quite well off really, with my pension coming in regular. It does get lonely sometimes though, for a Cockney, you can imagine. But then I can always go and have a natter with that Hugh and give a kick to his bloody old tombstone when I get really furious.'

Maisie talked and they listened, sitting side by side, their backs against the warm stone of the cottage, their eyes drawn towards the water which glinted beyond the hedge.

As they sat there, the day began its retreat. Jens, looking round him, could see a change in the light and the green foliage all around expand as it lost colour. 'I think we'd better be off. It will be getting dark soon.'

'Rubbish.' Maisie's hoot of laughter bounced off the sky. 'He doesn't know much, does he, dear? It doesn't get dark for hours this time of year. It'll be still twilight at half-past ten.'

'We had better be off, Maisie.'

'No – you stay and I'll row you back to the bridge. I don't have company that often and I enjoy a bit of exercise at night. Come on now – I'll put the kettle on again.'

So they stayed and drank more tea, and the air grew thick and honey-coloured. The cat came out from the house and purred around their ankles, pushing its head against their legs; Maisie's voice sounded from a distance and Pauline wondered if life could ever be as perfect again. Jens moved his arm to swat an insect and she felt the shock of his flesh against her hand.

'Oh yes, I loved that man. I really fell for that bloody Paddy.'

Emboldened by the twilight, Pauline did not look away as Jens's eyes met hers.

I don't care . . . I don't care any more . . . I really don't care.

The journey back was surreal. Pauline and Jens sat together, facing Maisie. She was a skilled oarswoman, sending the boat shooting through the water with barely a ripple breaking its brown, glass surface. There was a hurricane lamp on either side of her, and Pauline, staring, saw a queue of winged creatures waiting to commit suicide in the lamps' fiery hearts.

Beyond the river the flat countryside seemed augmented, released from the heat of the day. All around there were echoes like sighs and little rustling noises, as if it were settling itself down for the night. But the twilight would linger for a few hours yet, the memory of the golden sun, seeping into the landscape, would keep greyness at bay. In the fields, the ancient trees seemed completely dense, no sky showing through their leaves. They looked enamelled, unreal, trees in a picture.

Maisie left them at the bridge, helping them on to the road and pointing them towards the village. They watched, waving as she grew smaller and smaller, until eventually the light from the hurricane lamps was lost in the greater light of the sky.

'I should take your hand perhaps? It is not so easy walking in this light.'

She held out her hand and they swung along like children. They didn't talk and the silence lay between them – warm, like the evening. Pauline expelled a long breath and heard the countryside sigh with her, as pleased as she. The world was deserted, created for them, no beast nor bird abroad. Ahead, the lights of the village came faintly into view, and together, without consultation, they quickened their steps. Just another half-mile.

When they got back to the hotel, they found preparations under way for a dance that night. Already many of the guests had arrived and the Cocktail Lounge was crowded. Chairs and tables from the dining-room were stacked along the corridors and Mrs Flood, passing by, threw them a demented smile.

'Shall we have our nightcap upstairs tonight – it's so busy here.'

'Lovely.'

'I'll bring them up.'

'And I'll just . . .'

Pauline made her way to the Ladies. There was a vase of flowers on the table in the corner and someone had covered the wooden ledge that ran along under the mirror with a white tablecloth, folded into a strip.

As she stood putting on some make-up, two young girls came in. They were talking and laughing, unaware of her or indifferent to her presence.

'I'd keep an eye on Jimmy,' the smaller one said, winking at her friend in the mirror. 'Rose might prove stronger competition than you bargained for. I mean – that's some dress.'

The friend clutched at the wooden ledge for support, her body shaking with laughter. 'Oh my God, if she could only see herself and that neck like a plucked chicken. But,' growing serious, 'isn't it awful though what gets into women when they get to that age? I suppose they just get desperate for a man and don't realize they're making such eejits of themselves. You know,' she began to laugh again, 'I think Rose quite fancies herself in that get-up – even thinks she looks sexy!'

'I've heard she's good for a court in the back of a car anyway.'

They went out together, still laughing. Their perfume and cigarette smoke lingered behind.

Pauline put the lid back on her lipstick and dropped it into her make-up purse. She considered the tiny bottle of perfume sitting in front of the mirror but then swept it into the bag too. Fearfully she raised her head, forcing her gaze upwards. She wondered how, five minutes ago, she had failed to notice the bags under her eyes, the sag of her jawline. She had even been thinking she looked rather well, after her day in the sun.

Poor Rose. Poor Pauline, who couldn't even offer compensations in the back seats of cars or hotel bedrooms.

She put out her tongue at her reflection and snapped shut her bag. Courage and a measure of dignity and to hell with your bleeding heart.

Chapter Ten

All afternoon Jens had had a sense of approaching crisis. From the moment they had set out along the leafy canal walk, he could feel the charged atmosphere. The weather reflected his inner feelings, the heat heavy and still with the threat of thunderstorms in the air.

And then, that strange meeting with the old lady, listening to her as she talked on and on about her dead husband, and the boat journey back across the dark water. He wondered from where the crisis would erupt, not yet identifying and not wanting to identify Pauline as its possible source.

Since the evening that he had driven her to the hospital, Jens had thought of Pauline as a friend. And a friend was what he needed, isolated and bored in a country that was turning out to be much more foreign than he had bargained for. He had been reassured rather than disappointed by the absence of any sexual *frisson* in their relationship, putting it down to Pauline's forthrightness, her obvious lack of ambiguity. He found her handsome but unappealing, her shoulders too squared, her gaze too direct. In other circumstances he might have looked for something more, but memories of his long war with Helga were still raw and he was well pleased with what this woman seemed to present, not even piqued by her apparent indifference to his maleness. And because she offered neither threats nor promises, he was incurious about her, taking her as he found her.

Then, suddenly, when his eye was off her, she

changed. The brisk competence was replaced by something softer, less sure; the frank blue gaze became veiled and complex; the very lines of her body seemed to grow less angular and more pliant.

Aware of all these changes, he had not, however, acknowledged them to himself, and when, this afternoon, his mind had turned with faint uneasiness to affairs and all their messiness, he made no connection with the woman by his side. The worry, if that was not too strong a word, seemed merely an abstract one.

As the day progressed, he did become aware that there was something new, there, between them. He felt excited, but still uneasy, afraid of what was in the air. Then, sitting drinking tea and listening to the old woman's voice ringing out over the still water, declaring her love for her dead husband, he caught Pauline's eyes on him and realized with a shock that she was in love with him. He turned away, as much from his own confusion as from her nakedness.

However, on the journey back through the glassy water, listening to the scoop of the oars, watching Pauline's face, lovely in the moving shadows, he thought – what the hell! It would be worth it all. And soon he was feeling quite a lad, and younger and tremendously capable. He remembered the golden bloom on her skin as she had sat in the sun, the roundness of her thighs as she leant against the wall of the cottage. He recalled, too, the delights of sexual dalliance and, feeling a sudden rush of generosity, vowed kindness to her, kindness, gentleness and patience.

So he waited now, outside her bedroom door, the whiskeys growing warm in his hands. He noticed with interest that they were sweating – so much for experience and sophistication. He was prepared to share the joke with her afterwards; he was already looking forward to that post-coital interlude, the intimacy, the tenderness.

Her walk along the corridor was halting, shy. He had expected that. For the first time he began to wonder about her. Had she ever been married – had she had many lovers? Irishmen drank too much, he had noticed that, even in the short time he had been here.

She stretched out a hand and took one of the glasses, then manoeuvred herself so that her back was against the bedroom door. 'Thank you, Jens, this is lovely. I'll say good night now, if you don't mind. I think I'll have this in bed. It's been such a long day and I'm exhausted . . . I hope you don't mind.'

The door closed, gently, in his face.

Mind – why should he mind? In fact, stopping to think about it, the whole thing was fortuitous. He was lucky not to get involved, when his emotions were not really engaged, and with somebody her age it would be so deadly serious. She had saved them both embarrassment. He would probably have ended up by hurting her and he didn't want that. She was a nice lady, not very exciting, but nice.

In his bedroom he stared at himself in the badly placed dressing-table mirror. Was he losing his hair? And he *was* getting flabby. Perhaps he shouldn't drink that whiskey – he had been drinking too much lately. He felt suddenly dull and flat. The bedroom was stifling, but preferable to the noise and cooking smells which had rushed in when he opened the window.

He looked down on the yard with its empty beer barrels and rusting farm machinery. He did not really understand how the evening had turned out as it had. He had been so sure – how could he have misread the signs? Unless they did things differently in Ireland. Annoyingly, he felt a twinge of desire as he remembered her shining eyes, her look of beseechment.

Throwing his whiskey down the sink, he took up his toothbrush and began to brush vigorously. That was one very strange lady.

Next morning the sun still shone but there was a breeze blowing in from the countryside. When Jens opened his window, the air smelled of turf smoke and meadows. Now he thought of last night as an escape. It could all have been another ghastly muddle, especially with those expectations . . . He had seen her this morning, as he put his suitcase in the car, looking down at him, her face creased in anxiety. Perhaps she had feared that she was going to be deserted.

Pauline *had*, and without much surprise, remembering loutish behaviour from her courting days. Her spirits had risen at Jens's wave and, when she found him smiling at the breakfast table, all her misgivings disappeared.

'It's our last holiday breakfast – we must enjoy it. No, you must have more than toast,' he chided her. 'We have the journey and you do not look forward to my driving, I am sure.'

'But I do, I do.' Smilingly. But wait. This was *not* a flattering reaction from him – rather the reverse. He had been rejected: so shouldn't he be downcast, or at least sulking, not full of this early-morning bonhomie? He seemed relieved – very likely he *was* relieved. Oh God. She had probably thrown herself at him last night, left him no option.

Pretending to cough, Pauline hid her face in her paper serviette.

'You have caught a cold? I hope not, for summer ones are the most difficult to get rid of. Perhaps you should wear a cardigan?'

I don't want another mother, I can't even get rid of the one I buried six months ago. 'No, I'm fine, thank you. It's not really a cough, just something caught in my throat.' Shame, humiliation. You could choke on either of them.

'Then shall we be off? If I can help with your luggage.'

Mrs Flood stood on the steps and waved them goodbye. Otherwise the village was deserted. Shop doors were still closed and outside T. Donnelly, Fancy Goods, bundles of newspaper leaned crookedly against cartons of milk.

Ahead of them the road ran straight and white. 'It has been a good holiday,' Jens said, changing smoothly into

110

top gear, 'and thank you for being my guide. It would not have been so interesting without you.'

Pauline closed her eyes and settled back. It was seventy miles to Dublin. Perhaps they would both be killed before they got there, if the car went out of control, which was a commonplace phenomenon with cars, according to the newspaper headlines. Feeling the lurch of her stomach as they sped on, listening to the casual insolence of Jens's whistle, Pauline could well see this happening. And not such a bad exit, with that insolent requiem offering more solace than any nightingale. Futile to will the sun to shine, futile to wish to order one's life.

Pauline opened her eyes and smiled across at the handsome, smooth profile. Not only was she driving along in the shadow of death, but she had suddenly remembered that last night it was she, ultimately, who had said no. And if they ever did get back to Dublin, he must surely view her differently. Other fish to fry, he would speculate, as he remembered that final night in Flood's Commercial Hotel. For he couldn't possibly imagine . . . who could?

Looking down at her elegant leather shoes, her long legs, naked and tanned in the modern fashion, Pauline would not have believed it herself if it were not for her irrefutable knowledge.

As they approached the Curragh, Jens slowed the car. 'I find this a very interesting landscape, I should like to see something more of it. Shall we take a stroll?'

They turned away from the road and Pauline felt herself walking on top of a flat, green world. The unbroken line of the landscape gave her a slight dizziness so that she reached out and steadied herself against Jens's solid back. On the edge of the horizon a string of horses was riding out. At this distance they seemed almost motionless, as did the clumps of sheep, like so many daisies on the sleek green swards.

The openness and lack of scale gave the landscape a

111

minatory look, inhuman in its echoes of space and infinity. Pauline shivered and felt a raindrop splash on to her cheek. Above them the sun still shone, but at the other side of the world the riders and their horses had been absorbed into a blackening sky.

'Let's run to the car,' Jens took her hand. 'There is going to be a storm.'

They stopped at a pub, as much for comfort as a drink, but the pub offered them little cheer, unprepared as they were for the sudden downpour. Raindrops splattered on to the empty hearth and the barman snuffled and wiped his nose surreptitiously on the cuff of his shirt.

'Do you really want a drink?' Jens asked as they stood looking at the grubby velveteen-covered armchairs.

'No.' But I'd like to sit beside you, even over there, to put off the evil moment . . .

'I think we have changed our minds,' he turned towards the barman, 'if you will excuse us.'

The barman, amazed by such civility, stared after them, then philosophically hawked some phlegm up his nose.

Pauline's anxieties had returned. She felt a constriction in her throat, an itchiness all over her skin. By the time they reached the outskirts of Dublin, the rain had stopped but the world still dripped. They drove through the new outer suburbs that had already acquired a half-ruined air and came to Rathmines, sullen and choked with cars.

This was worse, far worse than the end of other holidays. Pauline dragged herself along to the lift, almost immobilized by the weight of her depression. She felt now an acute sense of loss and already a nostalgia for the holiday. She could sense the propriety, the separateness of city life settling round them as they were whisked upwards.

They said goodbye at their front doors and the click of well-oiled locks sounded in her ears like the knell of doom. What was the point of anything – holidays,

112

sunshine, life itself, when doors and coffin lids had to click fast and finally?

She was wondering whether a gin would cheer her up or drive her to suicide when the phone rang.

'Well, at last.' It was Una's voice. 'Where on earth have you been?'

'I've –'

'I rang this morning and at lunch time. I was just about to give you up.'

'I've been away.'

'Well, never mind all that now – I've got news for you. Marie Gunning is in hospital.'

'What?' For a moment Pauline couldn't think who Marie Gunning was. 'Oh, yes . . . but isn't it too soon –'

'She was found bleeding in a field with a knitting-needle sticking out of her.'

'Oh my God – did she try –'

'Obviously, poor little tyke. I thought you'd want to know.'

'Where is she?'

'Vincent's. They took her there by ambulance some time last night.'

St Vincent's Hospital loomed like a sea monster above the roads of low, suburban houses. Pauline gagged on the hospital smell, reminded of her mother's last illness, although that had been suffered in a different kind of hospital, old and due for demolition. Here the shining surfaces reflected efficiency, the solidity of the long, straight corridors proclaimed confidence. Although it was the visiting hour, silence hung upon the building, and those who walked the corridors seemed to do so soundlessly. The sigh of the lift was barely audible.

Marie Gunning, the porter told Pauline, had been moved from Intensive Care and was now in Ward 5 on the second floor. A nurse directed her to a bed around which bright, floral curtains had been drawn. Peeping through, she was surprised by the plain childish face underneath the fashionable haircut.

113

As if I were expecting a Jezebel.

Marie lay, tiny and motionless, covered up to the chin by a blue cotton bedspread. Her eyes were closed and her usually rosy cheeks pale and damp-looking.

'Is she –'

'Oh, she's fine now, quite stable. Of course she's sedated. She won't wake up, or if she does she won't know what's going on.' The nurse's dark, serious eyes were turned on Pauline. 'Are you a relation?'

'Just a friend.'

'I think her parents are still here somewhere. They've probably gone to get a cup of tea. They were in a terrible state – no wonder.'

The girl spoke with measured solemnity and Pauline guessed that she was very new, still at the stage of playing nurse.

'Thank you, Nurse.' She smiled at the pretty, scrubbed face. 'I'll call in again tomorrow.'

In the reception area, people sat around on low armchairs. They stretched and yawned and scratched their heads, as if it were morning and they were coming to in their own bathrooms. Worry and fatigue had broken down their defences and they looked with dazed indifference at the white-coated figures that moved among them with professional deliberation.

Pauline found Marie's mother standing in a corner, staring at a giant rubber plant.

'Mrs Gunning?'

The woman looked up at her, a fatter, older version of Marie. 'Miss.' Her voice was flat and she shied backwards, as if expecting to be hit.

'I'm so very sorry, Mrs Gunning.'

'Yes, Miss, and it's very good of you to take the trouble.'

Don't make me feel worse, don't make me feel more wretchedly guilty.

'Would you like a cup of tea, Miss? There's a place just round the corner.'

Mrs Gunning bought tea and two Cellophane packets

114

of goldgrain biscuits. She spooned sugar into her cup and then dipped the wet spoon in the sugar bowl for more. She sat with her head averted, not meeting Pauline's eye.

'At least she's out of Intensive Care, Mrs Gunning.'

Mrs Gunning stirred her tea without responding.

'I mean, that must be one worry off your mind.'

The woman raised her head, her slack body tautening and her eyes shining with anger. 'Do you know what she's done? Do you realize it, Miss? Then what's the point of talking about one thing being better than another? Nothing could be worse than this.' Some tea from her cup dribbled on to her coat. She looked down at it, then looked away without bothering to wipe it off. 'And I have to get the tea for them at home and I've nothing in the house but eggs. I can't offer Jim eggs – he hates them.'

Suddenly Pauline saw she had begun to cry. Tears poured down her cheeks, unheeded. She raised her face to Pauline, looking like a round, elderly baby.

'He's blaming me, he said if I was a proper mother it would never have happened. That I encouraged her because I was always reading women's magazines and I gave her money for style when I should have spent it on Masses for her immortal soul. If the Guards hadn't been there, he would have come in here and killed her.' She paused at the realization of another horror. 'But what will the Guards do to her? Dear God, Miss, will they put her in jail for what she's done?'

'Of course they won't, Mrs Gunning – sure she's only a baby herself. We must wait until she's completely better and then she will be offered help, Mrs Gunning, not punished.'

'Then she *should* be punished, for she's a wicked, wicked girl.' She put her cup down and began to button up her coat but, half-way through, her hands, dispirited, fell on to her lap. 'She was such a lovely baby, Miss, you've no idea. She was as good as gold. I always say that's why I had five more – Marie was such an easy child to rear.'

She expelled her breath in a long sigh and then slurped down some tea.

115

'And maybe he's right, maybe it is all my fault – but I couldn't be hard on her. She used to worry so much about things and when I'd see that little sad face, I couldn't bear it. I'd say – "Here, Marie, here's a pound, go and buy yourself a pair of fancy tights or something." Maybe . . .

'He used to get on great with her when she was little. He sent her to Irish dancing lessons and she used to do the steps for him in the kitchen when she came home. He was so proud of her. Now . . . I think he might kill me when I go home tonight. He's a man who never took a drink in his life but he's a terrible temper, especially against the evil-doer.'

Over their heads, the 15-year-old evil-doer was probably still asleep, breathing in the air, faintly antiseptic and chill.

'Would you like me to take you home, Mrs Gunning – unless you want to stay on.'

'I have to go home, Miss, I have the tea to get yet.' The summer evening was still and calm. Beside Pauline, Mrs Gunning bit her nails and wept and told her story in brief bursts. It was a banal little tale, predictable. Pauline listened while part of her mind registered the beauty of the evening. The sun was setting over Dublin and the light was golden, opaque. Pauline knew that it would be delicious to stand out in its gentle warmth, to feel its benignity on one's bare arms.

' . . . and he only ever wanted the best for her, he wanted to give her what he had never had. And he said today, Miss, that he wished to God she had died.'

The sun struck through the windscreen and Pauline lowered a sun shield.

'He won't feel like that, Mrs Gunning, once he's got over the shock.'

'Ah, Miss – you'll never understand a man like mine. His sister married a blackie years ago. They got married in a Registry Office in London and went off to live somewhere in Africa. That's over twenty years ago and my man has never had anything to do with her since. She

116

used to write but he burned the letters unopened. Once she called, I remember Marie was about nine at the time. He threw a jug of water over her and banged the door in her face. He said he only wished it had been boiling oil.

'And what's that compared to this – what's marrying a blackie compared to murdering your own baby? If *I* feel the way I do – how could I ever expect him to change?'

The Gunnings lived in a newish housing estate near the school. The house was neat but austere. Unique among its neighbours there was no fancy wrought iron around the door, no frills on the curtains, no ornaments in the windows or vases of plastic flowers.

'Will I come in with you? In case he's –'

'No, if you'd just stay and watch. I'll turn on the light in the hall if everything's all right. In about five minutes.'

Pauline waited. Within minutes a feeble light showed through the glass panel in the door. In the fanlight, a statue of the Sacred Heart gazed down and Pauline, starting the car engine, prayed, without any faith, that He might somehow help the family He had been set to guard over.

Chapter Eleven

In the chill of the flat, Pauline shivered. She plugged in an electric fire and then began to turn on all the lights. It was still bright outside but she did not want to be surprised by twilight.

In the bathroom, sitting on the lavatory, as she began to pass water, she felt a sharp pain imagining the sensation of cold steel plunging into her soft insides.

Mrs Gunning was right: whether the police brought a prosecution or not was beside the point – Marie was marked for life. And what was to become of the child? Could a father refuse to take in a minor? Could they all survive under the one narrow roof? Perhaps St Rita's could take her in.

St Rita's was an orphanage that Pauline used to pass on the way home from school when she had lived in Drumcondra. Nowadays St Rita's housed few real orphans but rather the children of broken marriages, of parents who couldn't cope. Pauline's eyes, travelling across the road, would collide with the high grey walls of the Hospice for the Dying. Around the corner, out of sight but often the cause of traffic jams in the narrow streets, was the cemetery. In the middle, where three roads converged, lay a dank and sunless park, a strip of weedy, dusty grass, always deserted, always in shadow. The little shops around, which sold fire kindling and children's toffee bars, usually had a profusion of fresh flowers. These were stuck in plastic buckets outside on the pavements, offering flashes of incongruous colour in the midst of all the grey. Colour to cheer up the dying and bury the dead.

Pauline used deliberately to choose that route from school, for once she had passed through that small, sad triangle and the car began to rise towards the canal, the rest of the journey, and home itself, did not seem too bad. But the thought of Marie tramping along those pavements every day made Pauline resolve, there and then, to take in the child if it were legally possible.

'Guilt,' said Mammy, making a sudden appearance at Pauline's shoulder, staring at her daughter in the bathroom mirror. 'You're not really anxious about the girl, you just want to make yourself feel better.'

'And is there anything wrong with that? Of course I feel guilty – what do you expect? Now go away and leave me alone – I'm going to bed.'

But she could not go to bed. She wandered round the flat, touching things, struck anew by the pointlessness of her life. She wondered what on earth she was doing in this flat, and then, what she had been doing out of it for the last few days. She couldn't think of Jens without a feeling of churning panic, an acknowledgement of her most damning and final failure.

And now there was a distaste for all things carnal, most of all for her own surges of emotion which she recalled with a blush. She wished she had gone to France, to paint badly and eat bread and garlic and to be dried, withered, purified by the fierce Provençal sun. She might have come back a spinster in spirit, as in station, and resumed a life of modest comfort with a happy heart.

In sudden fright she raced to the hall to turn off the light. If he should see it and ring the bell ... But the bell remained silent. Pauline, too sad to drag herself through the pre-bed rituals, gathered the bedspread round her and lay down on it fully clothed. Eventually she fell asleep, and dreamt, not of hospital and knitting-needles and gore, but of a seaside town in the west of Ireland where she had spent a holiday with her parents and brothers when she was eleven.

She woke with the tang of the Atlantic in her nostrils, the pounding of its breakers in her ears. The pleasure of the dream stayed with her, not retreating as it usually did before the assault of reality, and she jumped out of bed, suddenly hungry, as if the sea breezes were indeed whipping up an appetite.

There was nothing in the kitchen except an egg and half a jar of instant coffee. 'I'll have breakfast out,' she decided, seeing this as an extravagant, even exotic act, 'and I'll call for Una and take her along.'

Rory answered the door. His wiry black hair was sticking out round his head, the exposed temples naked and white. The back of his shirt stuck out too and his feet were bare.

'Sorry – am I a bit on the early side? I just thought –'

'She's in hospital.' He swallowed whatever he had been chewing and opened the door wider. 'Come on in, I'm having breakfast. Have a cup of tea.'

The little girls smiled at her from behind the table but they were busy fighting over a giant box of cornflakes.

'This place is a mess.' Rory pulled out a chair and examined it critically before he offered it to her.

'What's wrong with Una?'

'High blood-pressure, so the quack says. Took her in last night, no warning or anything, just like that.' He sighed, dropping a teabag into a mug and slopping water on top of it.

'You're not worried about her?'

'Of course not. They'll calm her down in there and she won't be able to run around like a lunatic, which was what she was doing here. She got into such a tizzy over the Gunning girl and then she got even more upset when she couldn't contact you.'

If anything should happen to her . . . but Pauline knew that this was an excess of foolishness. It was unlikely that Una would die just so that she, Pauline, should be punished. 'I'll call and see her this afternoon.'

* * *

121

Bewley's Oriental Café was crowded and smelt, as usual, of coffee. It was years since Pauline had been there and she looked around with interest. Mammy would have been scandalized at the idea of having breakfast outside one's own home, but Pauline guessed that it was an everyday occurrence for those people who sat around her. There were men, serious and pre-occupied, reading the morning newspaper. They dispelled any suggestion of frivolity and gave an air of purpose to the drinking of coffee and munching of toast. The women were thin and expensive, their eyes restless, faint frowns between the carefully plucked eyebrows.

Pauline chose a table beside the window so that she might look down on the passing scene. The figures below appeared to bob along, hurrying to get wherever they were going, brightly clad for the heat which was already making itself felt. The scene was shoddy and young and carefree. It was as unfamiliar to Pauline as the surface of the moon. A vitality emanated from the fusing mass, rose with the morning heat, and Pauline drew back, threatened. Catching her reflection in the glass of the window, she saw with dismay a well-groomed woman in early middle age. I'm being pushed out, she thought, I'm not part of them – the youth, the young – any more. I've been pushed over the brim and I'm starting the descent.

She looked around at the people in the café, at the men whose hands crept towards their bald spots as they read the financial news; at the women whose rigidity of back belied the snatches of carefree laughter.

Pauline gripped one hand to the other. How can we bear it, she wondered? Why are we not all screaming out in panic instead of sipping politely at cups of tea?

'God is good, maybe He'll spare me another few years,' she remembered Mammy saying, her body propped round with pillows, for without them it would keel over, a rag doll. She remembered the pouchy yellow skin, the mouth loose and pleading but the blue eyes blazing with life, clear and far-seeing, a young girl's eyes, incongruous in the decaying face. Coming into the hospital an hour after Mammy had died, Pauline had found that she looked much as before except for her eyes. They had lost their sheen, had become dulled and fish-like, so that the blue, so fierce in life, now seemed more grey, indeterminate. The ulcer on her leg still wept but the eyes had set in their jelly moulds.

Pauline felt an easing, like a cough that had softened overnight, as the thongs of hatred gave inside her chest. At last she had found something in common with her mother; they had, after all, inhabited the same planet, lived under the same shadow. Pity the mother, pity the daughter, pity us.

She had a sensation of suddenly looming faces, lips that moved and smiled, teeth that soundlessly gnashed. They zoomed in on her, with brows that were carefully plucked, chins that were tenderly shaved, mouths that were coloured red or pink. They zoomed in on her and she recoiled from those silently screaming, hideously painted, grinning skulls.

Sweat broke on her forehead and her hands were damp. She closed her eyes and breathed deeply, deeply, as Mammy had taught her to.

And then as she ran from the café and into the treachery of a July morning she found herself beginning to laugh. There had been so much self-approval in that upstairs room, so much purpose and commitment. I should go back there, she thought, I should go back there and give them a pat on the back. Or a wink.

That was all you could do with life – give it a wink.

Pauline wandered round the shops until eleven when she thought she might venture in to see Una. The hospital was shadowed and cool after the streets and Una was on the second floor.

'Turn left,' said the porter. 'Maternity right, observation and complications left.'

Una was knitting. She made the stitches like a child, grasping the wool between thumb and finger and hauling it round the needle. In the sunshine Pauline noted with a pang the scattering of grey over her dark, lowered head.

'I called to take you to breakfast in Bewley's and found Rory in command.'

Una's face brightened. 'It was such a fuss last night – I just had to walk out and leave everything.'

'They seem to be coping.'

'Of course they are, Rory's much more efficient than I am.' She raised her head and stared at Pauline. 'He's been great – he really has.'

'You don't have to sell him to me, Una.'

'I'm not a complete fool. Last night, it was very strange, but when I started getting the pain –'

'He didn't mention any pain.'

'We both knew how much we wanted these babies. And then I thought about Marie and I wondered why I imagined I had problems.' She heaved herself up and patted the mound of her stomach. 'I think they're having a football match at the moment. Do you want to feel?'

Gingerly, Pauline put out her hand. She felt as she had at nine years old when Raymond had forced her hand down on a mass of frogspawn.

'Here,' Una was smoothing down the nightdress. As Pauline's hand drew nearer she began to feel heat radiating upwards. She placed two fingers, gently. Nothing, then a pulse, then what could only be described as a kick, as if the tiny creatures inside were expressing outrage at the weight imposed on them.

Pauline sat back laughing. 'They are already expressing themselves forcefully, I see.'

'Can you imagine the time I'll have with them when they start to answer back?'

Pauline left the hospital and drove through O'Connell Street. On either side crowds strolled by and it seemed to her that every second woman she passed was pregnant, waddling splay-footed in loose, light-coloured dresses. Those who weren't pregnant were pushing prams.

Commonplace, ordinary, but beyond her.

On the way to St Vincent's she stopped to buy some

sweets, Mars bars and Polo mints. The doors of the ward were open today and she saw that Marie was sitting up, reading. Pauline waved and hurried forward but when she got to the bed, the girl's eyes were closed, the magazine discarded by her side. Had she been mistaken?

'Marie?'

There was a hardly perceptible tightening of her lips. Pauline laid the sweets on the locker, then took them up again. In the hallway, she threw them into a waste bin.

The child was right, of course, had more sense of what was fitting than she. The sliminess of her own gesture, arriving with her bag of sweets for smiles and chatter, struck her now, setting her teeth on edge. She had probably even been expecting gratitude from Marie, a recognition of her kindness in paying this visit.

The porter opened the glass door for her and she breathed in the unexciting air of the suburbs as if it were a mid-ocean draught.

But it was her own smell, not that of the hospital, that she was trying to get rid of.

When she got back to the flat, there was a letter waiting for her, from Raymond. He was writing, he said, to inform her that he was willing to let bygones be bygones. For the sake of their dead parents he was going to overlook her behaviour and, since he was coming to Dublin soon, he would like to call and see her and bring the children, who never stopped talking about their auntie.

The letter had been forwarded by her solicitor, Mammy's solicitor really. With difficulty Pauline tore the offensively thick paper into precise strips, then threw them into the kitchen bin and emptied tea leaves on top of them.

Closing the lid of the bin, she realized that she had recovered the sense of being in control of her life. The last time she had felt that was when she had shut the hotel door on Raymond. Since then, she had dithered.

Pouring herself a glass of water, she took it into the living-room where she sat with her back to the window.

She must take herself in hand and stop this adolescent behaviour. Since Mammy's death she had embarked on a series of abortive plans, deciding her future in this direction and then in that, beset by decisions and terrified of them. It was neurotic behaviour, and damaging not only to herself. Look at Marie. And even Una – she must be dizzy with her approaches and retreats.

As for Jens – but she couldn't think of Jens.

On the table in front of her lay her cheque book and she opened it now to examine the balance. Eight hundred and fifty pounds and this month's cheque due to arrive next week. There was also her savings account, with several thousand. So what was she doing mooning around Dublin? Summer was almost over and she had frittered it away without even noticing.

She would go to Florence, choose the most expensive package she could find and spend her holiday walking through its marbled galleries and museums. It was twenty years since she had visited Florence, hitchhiking there from Le Havre and staying in a youth hostel. On her back she had carried a knapsack full of books, and her head had been full of Art and Life. Now she would stay at an expensive hotel and eat delicious food in the evenings. It was not a totally tawdry exchange; she might even enjoy it if she stopped being such a prig.

'Grow up, Pauline,' she admonished herself in the bathroom mirror. 'You're maimed – so what? So is half the adult population of the planet. Life hasn't turned out as you thought it would when you were seventeen, but it's still here and still to be lived. So shut up and put up and stop baying at the moon.'

Directly she went to the Golden Pages and, choosing at random, began to dial the number of a travel agency. Within ten minutes she had booked her holiday: two weeks in a starred hotel, not in Florence but in cooler Fiesole, looking down on the city and with a limousine service to the *Duomo* every hour. Her room would have a balcony facing towards the city and she would drink her aperitif there in the evenings, watching the lights as they came on down below.

'People are starving in Africa at this very moment,' said Mammy mildly, sitting down on top of the Golden Pages, her expression concentrated as she chose a chocolate from her favourite selection. 'I'm sure you're quite right and it is your money, but I know I couldn't do something like that, at no time in my life. I would have been consumed with guilt. But then, we are so different in so many ways.'

'Yes, Mammy,' Pauline banged her fist on the table, 'quite different people. And besides, you're dead now, dead and rotten, so just shut up.'

Pauline jumped up and hurried to the bedroom. Opening the doors of her wardrobe, she looked inside with pleasure. Since she had cleared out the accumulated rubbish, every garment that hung there was one that she wanted to wear. For Florence she would choose the cool, the pale, the casual. Flat shoes for walking in, her prettiest dressing-gown for standing on the balcony in the mornings. She would not dress up, leave that to those who wanted to impress. She, a woman alone, would want to appear well dressed but not conspicuous. She would bring a hat and sun-glasses – no beachwear, and that was something to be grateful for. She might even –

She jumped as the doorbell pinged. Jens stood there, propped against the jamb, his briefcase supported between his ankles.

'You look tired.' She said the words without thinking, a reaction to his stance.

Perhaps he heard the concern in her voice for he smiled warmly and reached out to touch her hair. 'No, it's nothing. Just the traffic and a few problems. But how are you? I have not seen you since our return. I want to ask you to come out with me tomorrow.'

But Pauline had remembered by now and shame came rushing in. 'I can't go anywhere, I'm going to Florence.'

'What? Now?'

'No. At the end of next week.'

He laughed aloud, sounding genuinely amused. 'You are difficult to keep up with, Pauline, but I still think you might have time to come out with me tomorrow night.' He looked at the dress clutched in her hand. 'Is it not possible to take a night off from your packing?'

'Really, I –'

'It's my birthday. I'm fifty tomorrow and I don't want to spend it alone. Perhaps you don't feel like going out with a man half a century old.'

'Of course that's not it. Anyway, you don't look –' she gulped back the rest of the phrase. 'Sorry – I'm making a mess of this. Yes, I'd love to come out with you on your birthday.'

She tried to return her thoughts to Florence after he had gone, but it was difficult to concentrate. The look on his face – the opening up which revealed an unexpected rawness – kept coming back to her, causing her delight, despite her stern rebuke to herself. That the sleekness could be dented, the sheen dulled, brought him suddenly within her ken and filled her with tenderness. She felt it spreading, wobbling its way throughout her body, undermining her resolve. Tomorrow, she said, tomorrow I shall go into town and pay my deposit to the travel agent. Once that is done, I will be secure. And when I return from Florence, it will be time to prepare for school and this seditious leisure will have shrunk to nothing.

But though she set her alarm, she didn't go into town next morning. She lay in bed and stared at the ceiling, filled with horror at the prospect of having to choose a birthday present for Jens. Or whether she should in fact buy him anything. What did one buy for a man? More difficult still, what did one buy for a fastidious half-a-century-old Dane? She must not presume – that ruled out all articles of clothing, records and ornaments; on the other hand, she must not overdo the self-effacement, so bang went the standbys, socks and aftershave. Perhaps a book? Unoriginal, yes, but serious and impersonal.

128

And there was Alan Hanna's bookshop in Rathmines so she didn't have to go into town.

The book, two hundred pages on Viking Dublin with illustrations, lay on Pauline's sofa wrapped in pink-and-green paper. Pauline sprayed toilet water along her arms and turned to have a last look at herself. The pale brown dress was not new, but Jens had admired it and she saw now how elegantly it fell from her hips, how the material moulded but did not cling. Catching the anxiety on her face she tried to smile, but it was more a grimace, stiff and unconvincing. Wetting the tip of her finger on her tongue, she ran it along her eyebrows, then tucked her hair behind her ears.

If I keep my mouth open but remember not to drop my jaw, I should be all right.

She picked up the book.

Chapter Twelve

Three carpet-tiles across, she turned to flee as she listened in horror to the thump of music, the sound of raised voices from behind Jens's door. Then the door was flung open and retreat cut off.

'Hi! This way to the party.'

Pauline stared with a mixture of fear and hostility into the sunburned face. Ice-cream teeth, blonde hair in a pony tail; only the eye sockets, dark and creasing, suggested that she was more than seventeen. Pauline followed her down the corridor, feeling frumpish and overdressed. The dirty, Danish rat, the latter-day Viking, marauding into her heart with his tale of lonely birthdays. She should march in and hit him over the head with his terrorist ancestors, all £19.95 worth of them.

'Here we are.' The girl stood back, ushering her in with hostess-like solicitude. 'This is where the fun is.'

There were about ten people in the room. Pauline had an impression of pale, expensive sweaters and bodies that gave a hint of overweight. Only two women, thin and looking bored.

Jens walked over. 'And surprise for me, too, Pauline, arranged by my colleague's wife.' He nodded towards the blonde girl.

She came bounding across like a puppy. 'Sorry I couldn't include you but I couldn't very well ask Jens for a guest list now, could I? I'm Laurie, by the way, and that's my husband Jackson over there, the tall guy who's trying to make it with Peter's wife. And I didn't catch your name?'

'Pauline Kennedy.' Now why did she have to add the Kennedy, making it sound so stilted.

Laurie hadn't seemed to notice. 'Nice to know you, Pauline. Is that a prezzie? Give it here. I've stacked them in the kitchen and he isn't going to get to open them until midnight.' She pulled playfully at Jens's earlobe and then turned away from them.

They stared at one another across the space that Laurie's exit had created. Jens cleared his throat. 'Americans are so friendly.'

'Yes, they are. And extroverted.'

'Yes. You must have some wine.' And then as he began to pour the wine and Pauline felt the familiar sensation of failure creep up from her toes, he added, 'I am really sorry we did not have our celebration, just the two of us. I had been looking forward to it.'

And now everything is all right, Pauline said to herself, hiding her face in the glass. Even if I am ignored for the rest of the evening it doesn't really matter, the party will have been a success.

At ten o'clock food arrived from an Indian restaurant on the Rathmines Road. Pauline found herself flirting over the popadoms with Jackson from the USA.

'I've heard about Irish eyes but yours really do smile, you know that, Pauline?'

'Only when stimulated by much charm and intelligence.'

This is it, this is you, the new, laid-back Pauline Kennedy.

At twelve o'clock the presents were ceremoniously rolled in on a tea-trolley by Laurie.

'Thank you, Pauline, it looks like a most interesting book and so appropriate.' Jens kissed her cheek.

'They weren't all plunderers, then or now.' She kissed him back. 'Happy birthday, Jens.'

What problem was that? No problem that she could think of.

She left before Laurie and Jackson, not wanting to hang on, dangling around hopefully. Inside her flat, however, she felt such a surge of energy that she knew there was no point in going to bed or even sitting down to read. She must do something. Then she remembered the old standby for rainy Saturday afternoons at home – she would clean the kitchen. Mammy used to prescribe it, remarking that idleness was the ruination of a girl's face, searing it with lines and pouches of discontent.

Sadly, this little kitchen was spick and span. The tiled floor was unmarked, the oven looked as if it had never been opened. On the shelves, jars of spices and herbs had their seals still unbroken; raising agents awaited release from their plastic entombment. Pauline shoved the jars around a bit and tapped the crumbs from the toaster into a plastic bag. Then, on an impulse, she swept the jars into the same bag. She was never going to use them now and in any case they had probably gone stale.

Tying a knot in the bag, she clunked it after her to the front door. Jens was walking towards her along the corridor. 'Let me take that for you.' She watched as he made his way towards the disposal chute. Hands clasped in front of her, she thought: We could be married now, tidying up before we go to bed.

'They've all gone. I was just downstairs saying good night.'

'It was a lovely party.'

'Ours would have been nicer.'

In the sitting-room she offered him a drink but he said he would prefer coffee. When he took the kettle from her and kissed her mouth, she wasn't even surprised; she had known, since 9.21, that it was going to happen.

The bedroom smelled of summer rain and she turned to look out on the night before turning back to Jens. As she bent to unbuckle her sandal she thought: My stomach is calm and my hands don't tremble. Jens smiled at her and folded his trousers over the back of a chair. It was ordinary, domestic, nothing lurid or sordid in the scene.

The strangeness lay in its familiarity: she could have

133

been going to bed thus every night of her life. Her hands moved as surely as his; she returned his kisses without a trace of awkwardness. The defluxion of pleasure reached out to the pores of her skin and, while she enjoyed it, she recognized its prescriptiveness.

'Do you find me amusing then?'

'No, just something I thought of.'

What was overwhelming was that it was happening to her. Tomorrow, she would no longer be a freak. Marriage, it now seemed to her, had lost its status. It wasn't being unwed at thirty-eight that was a cause for pity, not any more, not even in Ireland. It was being unbedded.

She felt a rush of gratitude towards Jens and turned to kiss him, this time more gently. 'I love you,' I do, whatever it means – not living happily ever after, or imagining I see you on buses, but wanting to do things for you, to minister unto you – although of course I'll never let you know.

'I had better get something.' Jens half-rose, still holding her hand.

'No, it's all right.' She wasn't likely to conceive that easily at her age. And if she did . . .

It felt a bit like the dentist's, the weight, a sensation that she might break. Desire ebbed but she was undismayed. It got better, everybody knew that, and she felt she hadn't done badly. She hadn't cried out or told him to stop and he had sounded as if he was enjoying himself. She felt him turn aside and stretch; a tiny click and light flooded on to her face. She wriggled aside.

'I'm sorry,' he said, adjusting the angle.

She opened her eyes and found him staring at her. Be bold, Pauline act casual.

'Did I hurt you?'

Oh, he would make a wonderful lover, recognizing and responding to every twitch of her body.

'I think I hurt you in some way.' He sounded puzzled.

'No, not at all, I'm fine, grand.'

'But . . .'

She followed his gaze, down towards the pool of light.

134

The wretched lamp now shone on her thigh and on a ruching of sheet beyond. The sheets on Pauline's bed were always white, for she found the modern fashion in coloured bed linen rather vulgar. Now she looked at the red stain spreading like a flower over the white cotton. Scarlet, the colour of sin and shame.

'But . . . there is blood. Do you – is it . . . Pauline –'

She felt her whole body blush. Now he would realize, he would put two and two together and see that he had spent the last half-hour deflowering a middle-aged virgin. She could imagine his disbelief, then his pity, even concern . . . finally amusement.

He mustn't, mustn't find out. If he did, she would have to run away, hide herself from him for ever. 'It's nothing to worry about, Jens,' twitching the sheet aside with a careless gesture. 'There was a bit of pain too, but it's nothing to worry about. I thought it would be okay by now, but I've been to the doctor and it's not infectious. I mean, it's not Aids or anything . . . if there was any risk I wouldn't –' She stopped as she felt his body recoil.

He cleared his throat, then sat up. 'Yes. It is perhaps a good idea if you do something – if you see to it. And I,' he drew his legs up neatly and hopped on to the floor, 'I shall go home now. You must be tired, the day has been such a long one.' He was gone so quickly he mustn't even have waited to get dressed. She stuffed her fingers in her ears so that she would not hear the click of her front door.

The bed was cold, with an unfamiliar smell. Her body felt sticky and slightly sore. In the bathroom she washed herself at the sink, not having the heart to run a bath. In the kitchen she heated milk in a saucepan and, pouring it into a mug, topped it up with whiskey. But as she raised the mug and sniffed at the steam she remembered that this had been Mammy's nightcap. She threw it down the sink and, picking up the whiskey, gulped some down from the bottle.

Back in the bedroom she stripped then re-made the

135

bed. She opened the window to banish a foreignness that lingered. When she lay down, she slept, immediately.

Awakening late next morning, she was instantly filled with a realization of her folly. Indeed, how she could have thought for a moment that VD would have been more acceptable to Jens than virginity seemed, now, not mere folly but insanity. And her assurance that she was no longer infectious, as they had looked down together at the spreading stain, must have compounded her deceit and brazenness in his eyes.

Why hadn't she offered the obvious explanation, a period, just ending? It would have been simple, wholly believable; not very dramatic, however, and drama was what had seemed necessary last night, if Jens were to be distracted and her shameful secret kept.

And today, that seemed such a little thing. He wouldn't have laughed, not Jens. He might even have been touched, have taken her in his arms . . .

Pauline jumped out of bed. She would tell him the truth. She would go and knock at his door and not turn her eyes away or hide her face, but look at him squarely and confess her – what? No great crime, no failure even, merely the circumstances of her life.

She was singing in her bath. She noticed that her body seemed to have forgotten its experiences of last night: no pain, no visible signs of its changed state. She soaped it down, patted it dry and lovingly caressed it with cream, grateful to it again for its resilience. When the doorbell rang, she threw on a dressing-gown and ran, bare-foot, along the corridor. He had come back, he had left the office because he had somehow sensed –

'Oh, Rory.'

'Have you any orange juice?'

'Yes –'

'Come on then, I'll make us a buck's fizz.' He thrust a bottle of champagne under her nose and sidled past her towards the kitchen. 'I don't know if buck's fizz is entirely appropriate, but I'm sure they're going to set the bucks fizzing one of these years. That is, if all the bucks haven't been entirely emasculated by then.'

'What are you talking about, Rory?'

'They've arrived, the babies – at two-thirty this morning. They're a bit small, in fact one of them is going to have to spend a week or two in a glass box but they are perfect, thank God.'

'And –'

'And we're calling them Una and Pauline. Isn't it lucky now,' he paused as he kicked open the kitchen door and carried the drinks before him into the sitting-room, 'isn't it lucky that I'm not one of your male chauvinists. I mean, I don't give a damn about sons and carrying on the family name, although you'd be amazed at the apparently civilized males of my acquaintance who do. I'm delighted to have two more daughters. Imagine – five women! I'm beginning to feel like some class of pasha.'

It was late afternoon by the time Pauline got back from the hospital. As she parked her car, she looked around for Jens's but it wasn't anywhere in sight. Perhaps he was working late. Outside his door she paused, staring at the wooden panels, willing them to tell her something. The brown paint remained bland, its shiny surface giving nothing away.

Inside her own flat she walked to the kitchen, closing the doors as she went, shutting out sounds from the outside world. She had a life of her own, a separate existence, and there were things to be done.

But making a pot of tea for one and drinking it didn't take long. How could it be only half-past six? Her watch must have stopped. The clock in the bedroom showed that it hadn't.

Perhaps she should go out somewhere – he might be back when she returned. She must leave him a note, though, just in case she missed him.

The note was brief and factual. She wanted to talk to him; she was going out but would be back by nine. Pleased with its lack of hysteria, she sealed it in a white envelope

137

and thrust it under his door. He might not check his post-box.

She walked across two roads to the park. In the daytime this was a gloomy place, the tall, dense trees that rose inside the railings excluding sunshine and casting shadows over the grass. At this hour the lower rays of the sun crept in and the air was warm, the light meek. Pauline sat on a bench, facing the children's playground. It was deserted, a rag doll lying forgotten across a see-saw. At the other end of the grass a group of youths kicked a football; an old man walked a dog along the cement path.

The shouts of the young men reached her faintly, their raucousness absorbed by the trees; there was a stillness about the evening which suggested a cosmic holding of breath, a suspension of everything for the moment. Nothing ill could happen tonight; Jens had not been involved in an accident nor would he come across the hall to tell her that he was finished with her and never wanted to see her again. As she walked gently around the park and then around a second time, Pauline felt a calming of her spirits, a slowing and quietening of the tics and pulses inside her skin. Strolling home past the tall, terracotta brick houses, she found herself admiring white geraniums in a window box, a cat stretched on the warm stone of a porch. Looking out, she found no threat in the world, no fear lurking in doorways.

Her composure fled when she found his car still gone from the car-park. Running upstairs, too impatient to wait for the lift, she pounded on his door, then bent to see if her note was still there. There was no sound from within and in the gap between floor and door a black void. It was ten past nine. He could be away for hours; he could stay out all night. She could see now how people went mad, became drug addicts and alcoholics. She reached for the whiskey bottle but let her hand fall back. The whiskey might slow her reactions, anaesthetize some parts of her, but, like toothache, the pulse of her anxiety would persist.

But where were her resources, her skills at waiting? Hadn't she perfected these as she had lived through seasons and decades with Mammy? The wave of depression which swept over her was physical in its manifestation. She felt the weight of it on her neck and shoulders and a pain in her chest as the constriction spread. It was too late to wait.

She flew back the way she had come, down the stairs, out to the car-park. Her car sat waiting for her under the trees. She could go – where could she go? It was growing dark now, colour seeping from the world. In half an hour night would have re-established itself over the city streets and there would be menace on every corner. Rapists, muggers, junkies in search of a fix, they would all be abroad – the newspapers talked of little else. And Pauline's generation had learned tennis, not karate. Putting her keys back in her pocket, she pushed with her shoulder against the glass doorway. Her waiting was not over yet.

Pauline had already washed her hair and ironed two dresses by the time her doorbell rang. She felt strong and sensible this morning and took only a half-glance in the mirror before she went to answer the door.

'Hi.'

She found herself looking into the shining, slightly prominent eyeballs of Laurie, the American girl. 'Hello. Come in.' Pauline looked past her but nobody else stood there.

'I hope you don't mind my calling round like this, but I thought it'd be nice to get better acquainted, seeing as we're going to be neighbours.' She paused for a moment, seeing Pauline's expression. 'I guess Jens didn't get round to telling you with all the excitement, but he offered us the flat and we said, why not. It's plenty big for two.'

Pauline stood up. 'You stay here, I'll just go and get us some coffee.'

In the kitchen she let the cold water run over her

trembling hands, then splashed some on to her face.

'It was all a bit sudden, wasn't it?' she called, her back still towards Laurie.

'I never thought Jens was so impulsive, neither did Jackson. I mean, Jackson thought that they'd be working together for about a month, that was the arrangement originally. Jens was to set up the plant, then when everything was going smoothly, Jackson would come over and Jens would show him the ropes. Then yesterday morning – wham – "You're taking over, Jackson, I'm going home." I thought maybe he'd had bad news or something – did he say anything to you? I told Jackson I thought it was a funny way to behave and I don't think it's really fair on Jackson either. Jackson says I'm making a fuss, but don't you think he might at least have cleared out his flat? He just stuffed some things in his car, as far as I can see, and he's gone off to some place in Britain where he says he'll catch a ferry home.'

Pauline carried the tray into the sitting-room. There was a pot of coffee and an unsliced coffee cake.

'That looks real good. My momma told me that Irish ladies are great bakers. Her grandmother was actually from Ireland, we don't know exactly where but we think it might have been Tipperary.'

'Do you take sugar?'

'No, I use these.' Laurie dropped two tiny white tablets into her cup. 'But tell me, Pauline, do you know – was there something wrong? I don't want to start blaming the guy if there's some problem at home, but I don't know what the heck I'm going to do with all that junk in there.'

Pauline sipped her coffee. 'I don't think there was anything wrong, not as far as I know, anyway. He said goodbye and that he'd see me next time he was over. He seemed in good form.'

Chapter Thirteen

Pauline Kennedy, schoolmistress and spinster, is sitting drinking tea in a Grafton Street café. It is mid-September, another school year has begun, and Pauline is happy to be back in harness. The weather helps, sunny and crisp. This afternoon, walking down the avenue from school, she passed by the tennis courts and listened with pleasure to the familiar pat of the balls. They will probably keep the nets up now till the end of the month.

Una is on maternity leave and is being replaced by a girl who looks about fifteen. But what confidence! This morning she had suggested that there should be a non-smoking area in the staff-room and that they might like to change the milk to a low-fat variety.

The First Years, as usual, look smaller and younger than last year's lot.

There are few signs of autumn about, or maybe it just seems so in the sunshine. The strollers in Grafton Street are dressed for summer, bare arms and legs, Smartie-coloured frocks.

Pauline sips her tea, thinking that it must be a sign of middle age that she has begun to enjoy this middle-aged beverage so much. She remembers when she used to prefer beer at this time of the day. Her father had been a great tea drinker. 'Tea's my drink, any time of the day or night,' he used to say. His daughter smiles now at her memory of that ineffectual man. She remembers him as small and yellow and usually retiring out of rooms, escaping, where to she never knew. She seldom thinks of him nowadays, which makes her realize suddenly that Mammy has not made an appearance for over a month. And she, Pauline, has not thought about her in just as long.

May she rest in peace.

There is no percentage in resentment against the dead, it doesn't pay off. And besides, it is time to start taking responsibility for oneself. Pauline Kennedy laughs out loud, causing the young waitress to turn and look at her. She smiles at the girl, reassuringly. 'Just something I was thinking of,' and the waitress walks away, not at all reassured. With one stroke our heroine bounded free and sent Jens scurrying as far as he could from the Island of Saints and Scholars.

But such grotesquerie, such *grand folie*. Since that night, Pauline has stopped blaming Mammy, and now the cry 'It's all your fault' is as much a thing of the past as a pair of perpetually grazed knees.

She feels lighter without the rancour hanging round her shoulders, lighter and more whole. She must visit Mammy's grave tomorrow. She is glad now that she didn't have her cremated, although she had been sorely tempted to. For the last twenty years of Mammy's life, a major preoccupation had been where she would be buried. 'Not beside your father, that's full up with all those Kennedys dying off at such an early age. Perhaps somewhere beside the sea? And I'd like some nice trees, evergreens.' She had talked of graves as other women talked of hats, and Pauline had determined many a time that she would have her cremated and scatter her ashes over the four extant Gaeltacht areas of Ireland. Mammy had been a great and querulous supporter of Our National Heritage. But Pauline now sees that it *can* matter to a person where they are going to be buried and she is glad for Mammy, buried beneath the Dublin mountains looking out towards Dublin Bay. Her daughter has planted snowdrops on the grave.

For some days Pauline has been pondering whether she should write to Jens. She can get his address from

Laurie and she feels she might. She would like to tell him the truth; maybe some day they could laugh over it together.

Tonight, she has a date. He's probably married and out for one thing only, not that he's going to get it. Pauline has decided views on casual sex and she has no intention of risking VD. Anyway, she thinks the whole thing overrated. Maybe if she indulged more regularly she would develop a taste for it, but she doubts that. She believes that, as with oysters, the taste must be developed at a relatively early age.

She savours the last of her tea with pleasure and then beckons the waitress, who is still eyeing her suspiciously. She pays her bill, leaving a modest tip.

Then she stands up and walks towards the door, a handsome woman of thirty-nine – one who walks with some measure of serenity and assurance into the autumn sunshine.

THE END

Ellen
Ita Daly

'A startling first novel. Initially the charm, sharp observation and slight self-mockery are reminiscent of a Jane Austen heroine. By the end Ellen has become something far more sinister'
JULIAN ALEXANDER, LITERARY REVIEW

An only child of Catholic Dublin parents, Ellen was a strange, solitary girl. She was lumpish and dull, she was lonely. But she had resigned herself to this, and wanted nothing more from life than to be left alone in her isolation, to carry out a quiet typing job without interference, without change. If only her mother would stop entertaining such ambitious fantasies for her. When Ellen's hopes of an academic career fell through, Mrs Yates moved on to visions of a glittering social success, inviting strange girls around for elaborate teas and friendships which never materialized.

Then Ellen met Myra. Pretty, rosy Myra who wanted Ellen to be her friend, to meet her family, to share a flat! A new world unfolded, a world which Ellen found completely voluptuous; evenings by the fire, fish and chip suppers, secrets shared with a friend – even if that friend could sometimes be casually brutal. Throughout the summer months, there were lazy days spent in the garden with Adrien, Myra's stockbroker boyfriend and his cousin. Bobbie even paid attention to Ellen. She had never imagined that life could be like this, and she wanted it to go on forever. Who would have thought that the idyll could be violated – let alone in the shocking way it was?

'A first novel that is formidably subtle and fluent'
GILLIAN SOMERVILLE-LARGE, THE IRISH TIMES

'An intriguing and disturbing picture of a moth in the glare of a flashlight'
COSMOPOLITAN

'ELLEN is a deftly promising first novel'
CHRISTOPHER WORDSWORTH, THE GUARDIAN

0 552 99251 8

BLACK SWAN